Bastion bounded around Ben's head. The beast whipped the black Nilosian energy there into a whirlpool which flash-flooded the vision away.

Annoyed, Ben snapped out loud at the creature in his head, "What?"

They didn't actually share a language. Bastion felt primal. It probably wasn't even capable of words. The only time they had any form of communication was during the combat with the ogre magi, when Bastion motioned to Ben before pulling him in.

Ben stiffened. Bastion only reacted to combat.

ADVENTURES OF BENJAMIN BAXTER: SAMHAIN SHENANIGANS

Book Two of The Darkness Within Trilogy

EZEKIEL JAMES BOSTON

ELSEWHERE
E
P
PUBLISHING

Adventures of Benjamin Baxter:
Samhain Shenanigans

Copyright © 2015 by Ezekiel James Boston
All rights reserved.

Published 2015 by Elsewhere Publishing
www.ElsewherePublishing.com

Cover art copyright © 2014 Irineo Maniego

Book and cover design copyright © 2015 Elsewhere Publishing

ISBN-13: 978-1-62538-053-1

Elsewhere Publishing
www.ElsewherePublishing.com

Dedicated to:

Family & Friends
Mentors & Minions
Kay McGarvey

EZEKIEL JAMES BOSTON

THE ADVENTURES OF
BENJAMIN BAXTER
SAMHAIN SHENANIGANS
BOOK TWO OF THE DARKNESS WITHIN TRILOGY

Chapter One

SAMHAIN SHENANIGANS

BENJAMIN BAXTER TOOK A DEEP INHALATION. Even though the large starwise only parking lots were full, the distinct Samhain Festival buttered popcorn smell extended all the way out into starwise overflow parking amongst the mundanes—the magic-less.

He licked his lips, and flipped the switch to close his coverable top.

Thrilled cheers rose in the distance. A round of faint applause chased it across the parking lot. Wondering what trick had been performed, Ben turned his attention toward the lit entrance so far away beyond rows and rows of cars.

Hoping to catch some remnant of the prestige, his gaze crawled along the Ferris Wheel, the Thompson Twister, The Screaming Meemie, and the various tents that filled the span between the rides.

Nothing. He snapped his fingers at missing it. *Well, they'll be more performances. That's for sure.*

The simple red, white, and dark lights of the festival

held his interest in a way that the millions of Las Vegas casino lights blinking for attention never could. Only the *click, click, click* of his closed convertible top gear over cranking pulled him from the momentary entrancement.

One of the largest gatherings for Samhain Shenanigans in the country, the festival pulled every student from the Vegas Valley and thousands of students from schools from nearby prefectures.

With all the practitioners here, I shouldn't be surprised that starwise parking is stuffed. Ben took a moment to center his red Archon Private Academy tie and got out of the car. He put on his tan A. P. A. trench coat to cover the huge star belt buckle of his Meadows Towing Might-Fist belt, and buttoned it closed.

He dusted one shoulder and then the other to activate a minor prestidigitation. A swift breeze whooshed down his body as the wrinkles in his clothes flattened out.

His mind went back to the popcorn. Every year, since he had the free first-year's serving, he wanted to get a bag, but had always opted for a hot pretzel, garlic cheese knots, or cotton candy.

Not this year.

This year he had a plan.

He'd do a few games to fill his pockets with prizes before grabbing a bag of the buttery good stuff and casually munch on it as he strolled through the festival. Then he'd return each of following nights through Halloween for more games and treats.

The keyword for this year's festival? Moderation. Slow and steady fun. Prolong the experience. Tonight would be great. Each night would be great so long as he stuck to his plan.

An odd tingling—*magic*—settled across his brow. A nearly overwhelming urge to take off his tie and leave it on his windshield washed over him and faded.

Ben scanned to find the source.

Two girls in Sunrise Mountain orange blazers, white blouses, and orange-and-white plaid skirts focused on him. One, dark haired, sported long pigtails. The other, a blonde, had her hair cut short like a pixie. Later than Ben to the first-night events, they'd had to park even further out in the mundane lot.

The brunette didn't have the thin orange tie to complete her school uniform. She locked eyes with him and moved to get closer.

Bastion—the monster locked away in Ben's head— roared and slammed into his temples. The beast tried to force its way through the bond that linked him and the monster together. It wanted to tear the girls apart.

Ben set his will against Bastion and wondered if he had been wearing one of the red, white, and black Samhain Shenanigans-logoed armbands to partake in the evening's school-pride scavenger hunt, would he still have been able to resist the girls' spell?

Bastion knocked around his head

Denying the beast's horrible desire to materialize proved taxing. Ben gave a strained smile and frequent grimaces broke his grin. "Sorry, girls." He patted the part of his arm where the participation band would have been if he were in play. "But I'm not in on The Shenanigans."

The brunette gracefully slid to close on him.

Ben backed away.

She gave a momentary pout before flashing a flawless smile. "Can I have your tie anyway?"

He shrugged. "It wouldn't be worth any points."

Temptation dripped from her playful lips as her tongue ran between them. "Can't you imagine me with your tie on?"

The magical tingling on his brow came back strong before fading out again.

A vision of a girl wearing his school uniform came to mind, but not the temptress in front of him. In his vision, Penelope stood in Pepperjacks with his trench coat on. A sole lower button held it closed. Besides his tie, he didn't know what else she had on under the coat, but wanted to find out.

Bastion slammed his temples again.

Ben grimaced. He stopped nodding to his imagination and switched to shake his head. "No. No, sorry."

This time, her pout stuck and her blonde friend pulled her away. "Let's get to the big top." She gave Ben a playful sneer, the kind that causes those cute little nose wrinkles. "We're bound to find *friendly* casters there."

Even as she was being dragged away, the brunette steepened her hands and lipped, "Please."

Ben gave a regretful smile.

She turned and fell in stride with her friend. Their skirts swung in unison for a few seconds.

The tie and trench coat vision flashed again. It had been almost a month since his run-in with Penelope. Ever since then, the hot, raven-haired beauty from the other side had become a constant in his dreams. Except for this recent vision, the Dream-Penelope still wore burlap. The bruises and scabs were healed, but her cutting blue eyes kept their edge.

He hadn't even notice the color of the Sunrise girl's eyes.

Faintly, Ben registered people yelling. He almost turned, but continued to the fairgrounds. Penelope crawled back into his mind and he focused on the memory. What had she worn after changing out of the makeshift bag-dress at Pepperjacks?

Reimagining her running for her life, a scaled hand closing in on her long, dark, trailing hair. Again, her intense blue eyes stole his focus.

Bastion bounded around Ben's head. The beast whipped the black Nilosian energy there into a whirlpool which flash-flooded the vision away.

Annoyed, Ben snapped out loud at the creature in his head, "What?"

They didn't actually share a language. Bastion felt primal. It probably wasn't even capable of words. The only time they had any form of communication was during the combat with the ogre magi, when Bastion motioned to Ben before pulling him in.

Ben stiffened. Bastion only reacted to combat.

From a ways behind him, a vaguely familiar voice called, "Yeah, we're talking to you!"

Ahead, the girls dropped their playful walk and sprinted toward the carnival entrance.

Undaunted, Ben turned. He registered three bodies in hoodies—*Dunn-Blatt or Clark costers*—beyond three small, snapping green energy hooks shooting at him.

Each hook trailed a wisp of emerald power back to one of the three hooded casters.

He dodged one.

The green hook flew past him. The faint line of energy dissipated.

Ben twisted. Too late.

The other hooks hit him in the center of his chest.

The faint lines of energy—challenge tethers—shone brilliantly as they twisted, strengthened, and locked Ben into a magic duel.

Chapter Two

HOOKED

AMBIENT DIMENSIONAL ENERGY flowed into the fetters binding Ben to the challengers. Not a valid target for the night's game, Ben didn't struggle for the dominant caster's advantage. Instead he focused on the subtle rush that came with being in a duel.

Just under his skin, the hook dissipated when the emerald strands solidified and thrummed as though some great entity strummed to test the sound. A heightened sense of awareness—the rush of air bringing intoxicating scents from the food court, distinct *clacks* of the Bull Dog speed coaster carts being tugged up toward the first summit, that vague knowledge that nearby, other wills were pitted against each other—came to him.

Ben rubbed the growing heat in his chest. The feeling spread into his hand. He stroked his neck and, like a topical cream, the warmth spread there, too.

Neither challenger noticed his lack of a participation

band. The two hooded casters had turned toward one another and, in unison, said, "Let go."

Ben had watched Jameson Brown's exit interview when the World Dueling Federation forced him out for not having won any of his first twenty-five professional matches. When the interviewer had asked Brown why he kept competing instead of quitting from embarrassment, he bounced in place like a jacked-up aureole addict. "The better the competitor, the better the buzz."

As though plugged into the world, Ben finally understood. His eyes narrowed in suspicion. Bastion had relaxed. *Why?*

The shorter one pushed the other. His voice an angry squeak. "He's mine!"

The last thing to come to Ben through the tethers, the challengers' intent. Ben found himself become even more nonchalant about being hooked. These two were at war with each other. Being connected to both, Ben could feel the deep-seated disdain between them.

This play for perceived power further unfurled as the taller guy pushed the smaller one back. "Let go."

From the voice, the taller caster had been the one who called out to him. Ben shook his head. Both were so petty and desperate to scavenge for Samhain Shenanigan items.

The smaller guy pointed to the tether in his chest. It pulsed a pale, neon green. "My hook hit first!"

The taller one grabbed the other by the collar. "Let. Go." He shook the smaller boy hard in time with each word.

Ben had been hooked for the first time three years ago when he'd just turned thirteen and had to take Adept Love's *Intro to Dueling* class. Malcolm—a bully—whose birthday fell nine months earlier, had tethered him. The hook felt like a real fishhook forced into his skin. Though there wasn't any blood, the pain burrowed cruelly up his arm before tearing to the center of his chest. Ben had dropped to a knee and struggled to keep from tearing up. Nothing would've been more embarrassing than crying on his first day of Dueling.

Before Adept Love had made it over to them, Malcolm had towered over him, mumbling insults about Ben losing his birthday gifts from the school and calling him a baby for crying, even though he had successfully held back the tears.

The taller boy jammed his knee into the smaller one's crotch.

The smaller boy collapse, but clung to the tether.

If being hooked would always remind Ben of Malcolm, he'd have to do something extreme to change it. But what?

Ben had often wanted to get back at Malcolm, and had formed several plans, but the bully had been kicked out of the Archon Private Academy. The faculty didn't say why, but since Malcolm often hooked sixth and seventh graders, it had to be for *conduct unbecoming of an enlightened individual*.

The tether from the small guy faded away.

Competition between them done, the intent of the guy with the remaining fetter came through clear. He wanted to do permanent damage and take as many scavenger hunt items as he could instead of obeying the mandatory limit of one per duel.

Though not a part of the multi-school event, Ben loathed bullies. He walked down the tether toward the hooded figure towering over the one on the ground. Closer, the purple and black of hooded zip-ups became apparent. *Dunn-Blatts.*

The victor flexed over the downed one and had been speaking softly. He spun to face Ben. "Give up four items, Ape, or I'll break you and take your car."

That snide tone. *No way.* Ben leaned to the side to see into the dark hood. Magical shadows kept the face in darkness. Ben's throat constricted with growing rage. "Malcolm?"

The tall boy pulled the hood back. "Baby Ben!" The magical darkness around the face vanished. Much taller and skinnier now, that same aggravatingly smug smile still haunted Malcolm's stupid face. "Do you still cry when hooked?" He chuckled and pointed. "Look, boys, I think I see tears starting."

Ben's fist balled. A primitive desire—*smash that hooked nose*—went through him. His muscles tightened. The direction of power through the fetter between them changed. Energy flowed in Ben's favor. To assure every iota of his anger would be felt, he projected his menace through the tether. "We've a score to settle."

That only add fuel to Malcolm's smugness. "Oh." Malcolm glanced to Ben's arm, where the Samhain Shenanigan's band should have been. "You aren't in the hunt?"

As the one challenged, it was up to Ben if he wanted to end the duel. Adept Love had chirped endlessly about that rule and, by Ben's count, he had three years of anger and two fonts of magic to unleash on the bully.

He held tight. "You're not getting off that easy!"

Malcolm blew him a kiss then extended his hands palms up. As if cued to the motion, two mystic whirlwinds appeared.

One next to him.

One next to Malcolm.

The swirling vortexes siphoned power from their tether. Wind flapped loose, dull gray robes, signaling the imminent arrival of Primaries.

No! Ben opened his Argosian font to try and blast Malcolm with pure power, but his energy drained off to the forth-coming Lesser Judges without so much of a flash of color. He closed his font.

Hoods drawn, both appeared in the thick official robes of the Las Vegas Magistrates. Each teleported into being with their two feet long battle rods—the true symbol of their power—at the ready.

The tips of their batons crackled with red energy as the two dour Argosian men scanned the area for greater trouble.

A third set of robes flapped. In an instant, the wearer materialized. She wore the same dull gray uniform, but her rod hummed with orange Vibrosian energy. Without taking time to appraise the situation, she demanded, "What is going on here?"

The third Dunn-Blatt—Ben had forgotten about him —helped the one Malcolm kneed to his feet. The three of them kept silent.

Ben struggled to keep a civil tongue and found himself at a lack of words. Anything he might say would be hash and pointed at Malcolm. His personal limit met, Ben kept his mouth shut. Actions could be explained away. Words could be quoted, and if he opened his mouth, he'd only regret it when the grey-robed Magistrates reported it to the head of his school.

The vibrant orange glow on the tip of the baton dimmed. She gripped it with her free hand and looked them over. "Junior Apprentice? Bravados?"

Malcolm tried to loosen the hook.

Holding it tight, Ben rocked with the small mystic tug in his chest.

Malcolm said, "A simple misunderstanding, Primaries." He shot Ben a *be cool* wink—as though things could ever be cool between them—and gave another tug. "I, along with my Junior Bravados, thought this A. P. A. student was in on The Shenanigans."

Ben shook his head slightly and held the tether.

Malcolm tugged again and narrowed his eyes. "It's become obvious. He isn't."

"You do not have an armband, Junior Apprentice." The Vibrosian Primary pointed her battle rod at Ben. "Release the Dunn-Blatt or risk censure."

Wishing the fetter would whip to slap Malcolm across the face, Ben relaxed his will and muscles. The hook came free. Without flair, the tether between them dissipated.

Malcolm's hand stashed something into his pocket. Probably his tether totem.

Ben's jaw tightened. Was the totem still the same rusty nail Malcolm had used to hook him years ago?

Smiling at Ben's building anger, Malcolm rubbed his

hair opposite the Magistrates with his fingers crossed. He gave a small laugh. "Sorry about that, friend."

The energy faded from the Primaries' battle rods. The two Argosian Primaries spun a quick circle. Air sucked from where they were headed, their gray robes flapped a cotton candy smell before they teleported. Small pink and pale emerald dust devils swirled together in the lot where they once stood.

The Vibrosian Primary turned to Malcolm. "Be careful where you throw your hook, Bravado."

"Yeah." Ben did not want to say anything, but found his mouth echoing the Magistrate as he continued to stare at Malcolm. "*Be careful.*"

She pointed her rod at Ben as an unspoken warning. *Behave,* it said.

He continued to stare at Malcolm and a light thumping in his head—Bastion—urged him on.

The Magistrate angled her wrist back and directed it at Ben a second time. Another unspoken warning. *You are not behaving.* An orange glyph lit the tip. "Look elsewhere, Junior Apprentice."

Ben looked up into the night sky. The light pollution from the casinos stole the grandeur. He focused on the North Star, wishing he could call it down to slam Malcolm deep into the earth.

She said, "Now, to the fairgrounds, you three. Be vigilant. Have fun."

Holding his position, Ben felt them walk past.

The first one, the tallest—Malcolm—bumped his shoulder as he passed, whispering something too low for him to catch, but what Ben thought had been said —*lucky baby*—burned in his ears and sent Bastion tromping its rage through his head. Ben struggled to find his center.

As much as he wanted to go at Malcolm, he had to keep his cool lest the Primary ban him from this season's festival. Still, his rage continued to build...

Chapter Three

USELESS WORDS

A DISTANT ROAR of excitement rolled from the fairgrounds. Though curious, Ben ignored it and let his eyes wander from the North Star through the rest of the Little Dipper. Having birthmarks in a similar pattern on his face, spanning from one cheek to the other, Ben always thought of it has *his* constellation. The fading smell of cotton candy piqued his desire to get onto the fairgrounds again, but he had to wait for the—*high and mighty, power-tripping*—Magistrate to excuse him.

She finally snapped her fingers for his attention.

As he supposed, unless he wanted to be booted and be in trouble when the next school eighth began, Ben faced her and granted immediate eye contact.

Vibrosian energy flooded her eyes.

Ben looked into her orange orbs. He'd only seen one other caster—Ur-Krurk—do this when the ogre magi wanted to blast him to bits. Could this protector, one of Las Vegas's regulators, be thinking of doing the same to him?

The magic drained from her eyes revealing brown irises. She asked, nearly demanded, "What were you thinking, Junior Apprentice?"

Filling his mind with the void between stars, Ben blanked his thoughts to block having them read. Before learning about mind reading a month ago, he had always thought the reactions of others coinciding with his thoughts intriguing. Now—*like G. I. Joe would say*—knowing is half the battle.

She inched forward, paused, and looked deep into his eyes. Concern eased into her voice. "*Were* you thinking?"

She didn't insist on him answering the first question. Keeping his block in place, Ben nodded.

Her fists knuckled her hips. Indignant, she asked, "How did you think you would fare against three Dunn-Blatts, here, in the parking lot?"

Ben continued looking into her eyes. In a blink, he steeled his thoughts.

The Magistrate's lips parted, and she failed to fully suppress a startled gasp.

"No offence meant, Primary, but my personal trials and battles are mine alone." Bringing his Courtmanship studies into play, Ben bowed fifteen degrees. The perfect angle to ask for permission from any caster not directly over him. "By your leave, Ma'am."

With annoyed wrist flicks, she waved her baton under his face to dismiss him.

He turned and walked toward the festival.

Flapping cloth—her teleporting away—sounded behind him.

The long walk ahead of him, Ben's mind kept going back to her baton waving before his eyes.

Ben's parents forbade him from dueling. Heck, they had objected so strongly—to his great embarrassment—at the Arcane Private Academy, where he went to learn magic, that the school excused him from their minimum dueling requirements.

As such, he had only witnessed the baton—a widely accepted symbol of social standing, enforcement, and personal power—from a distance. This close to one, he became certain he'd seen a similar rod fairly recently, but it hadn't been in a Primary's possession...

A replay of the Magistrate's baton waved before his mind's eye. He stroked his chin, murmuring thoughtfully to himself. "Where've I seen one of those before?"

Chapter Four

MUNDANE PROBLEMS

HIS ABSENT GAZE only a few feet ahead of his black dress shoes, Ben made sure to keep them clean by avoiding the hastily lain chalk lines in the mundane overflow lot. His thoughts bounced between jerk-faced Malcolm, the hot Sunrise Mountain girls, and the misplaced memory of a Magistrate's battle baton.

The rough gravel lot gave way to smooth blacktop with uniformly spaced parking spots separated by paint instead of chalk. The swells of thrilled crowds grew steadily louder as he closed on the fairgrounds from the mundane overflow lot, to regular mundane parking, and now, closer still.

Absentmindedly, his hand played across the thick bundle of Magic Fair winnings in his pocket.

A proud smile formed on his face.

He gave the wad a conscious squeeze.

Placing in the Junior Apprentice / Apprentice group brought five times the reward as the Initiate level, and had netted him more tickets than his prior six years of prizes combined.

He had earned seventy-two tickets. Two for participating, twenty-five for Grand Prize in Efficient Construction, another twenty-five for Grand Prize in Circuitry, ten for second place in Spell Programming, and a bonus ten had been bestowed upon him for taking the fair's Outstanding Ingenuity award.

The judges had gawked over the circuit board in his spellcards. They couldn't seem to get over the overwhelming simplicity of him having moved the arcane resistors closer to the thin obdurium strip. Between that and working the path of his printed circuits from the obdurium he had made the card need less arcane wattage to activate.

About to envision what the large Junior Apprentice prize plaques would look like above his smaller Initiates awards, voices—*either unhappy or pissed*—rose from the joyous background buzz.

Ben lifted his gaze from where the white parking lines ended, and froze.

The *Shame on Sam Hain* protesters were back this year. He counted the twenty of them. Their numbers would swell over the next two days.

These people were why Ben came before Halloween. Anyone coming too late on the actual All Saints Day would find this group impossible to wade through. Worse yet, the mystique—the buffer that kept most of the mundanes from seeing magic and magical beings— would be stretched so thin that they'd be able to see any nearby caster.

Ben waited.

A few of them looked around, scanning over where he stood.

As long as he remained still, or only moved when they weren't looking his direction—*perhaps if I creep very slowly...*—he'd go undetected.

Most were in idle conversation. All of them held large signs usurping the glory of the spindly iron wrought Samhain Festival entry arch. They protested the festival with *Bring Back Orange And Black* and *This Halloween is Not What it Seems.* They also railed against its main organizer, Sam Hain, with *Shame on Hain* and *Hain is Insane.*

Three years ago, as the new President of Koffman's Clockworks, Hain took control of the festival. His change in theme colors from brown and orange to traditional red, white, and black—for blood, bone, and ash—brought more magic-users to what had become, arguably, the best Samhain festival in the country.

Ben looked back over the chocked-full parking lot. Cars whizzed down Sunset Drive. Several sets of headlights moved through the overflow lot to find a spot, but no one walked toward the entrance. *I really should've come earlier.* Ben pressed his lips together, took a deep breath of the popcorn-laced air, and mentally prepared to interact with the Mundanes.

Ready to trudge through, he took one step.

"Don't go in, son!" A rotund man in a loud, orange, Halloween-themed button-up shirt locked eyes on Ben, and waved a *Red, White & Black Is An Attack* sign at him. His voice deep and serious, the man continued, "The Koffman Corp is slowly turning this festival into Devil worship."

Ben entertained a whim about sharing the true origins of the Pagan holiday. *How much would this guy freak out if I went into the details covered in Adept Roman's two Hidden History courses?*

Neither of the classes had a lick of magic. Ben had wanted to skip them, but he fell into the three percent of students attending the Archon Private Academy who didn't come from Pagan families, which made taking both mandatory. Like *Spell Programming*, *Hidden History* had ten levels that spanned multiple school eighths, but he didn't know anyone going that route.

Ben nodded and arced to walk around.

The man pressed closer. He smelled like pastrami.

Ben began to arc wider.

Turning the sign around, the man waved a red, white and black *Hain Is Heinous* at him. "Don't you see?" The man's hot breath reeked of coffee. "Hain is trying to shape the holiday into something wicked."

Ben kept arcing to the edge of the entrance like a slow-motion soccer ball hooking toward the goal pole. *Hope I hit the net.* "Sorry sir, but I won tickets—"

"I'll buy them from you!" The closer they go to the white chalk line marking private property, the faster and louder the man spoke, "Just don't go in!" They reached the white chalk line marking the threshold to private property. "How much you want for them?"

Noticing his angle would be off from making it across at the entrance, Ben stopped.

The man did, too. He thumbed through a wad of mainly black and green ink on gray paper; mundane money.

Scanning the substantial number of—*they're called*

dollars? Yeah, dollars—for the red on white *forge-strong notes* backed by the Anvilsmith Dwarves, or the orange on pink *monetary units* issued by the Sunrise Mountain Sisterhood, Ben saw none.

Having been raised as a Mundane until the age of ten, Ben had nearly forgotten just how much it would take to turn dollar bills into real currency. A term —*pennies on the dollar*—came to mind. *What were pennies again?* The exact meaning lay lost in his childhood memories, though he figured the exchange rate would be similar. Suddenly, he grasped that the man thought he would be purchasing regular ride tickets. Embarrassed at his own belated realization, Ben's cheeks began to warm and he grinned at how dim he felt. *Why would a mundane think of anything besides mundane attractions?*

Ben took a quick step to cross the thick line.

Trying to keep pace, the man moved, too. Some of his money threatened to come loose and the man paused to pinch the bills.

Just enough hesitation for Ben to take the final two steps across the line. "Sorry, sir." He turned and bowed a small courtly apology before walking backward. "But I really need to win some goldfish."

Chapter Five

CONJURER'S COURSE

CHEERS ROLLED from the opposite end of the midway games, near the entrance. The air positively brimmed with excitement. Ben had been hoping the attendant with Cody on his badge at the Conjurer's Course would share some of the fragrant spiced apple cider on a slow simmer in the booth, but he hadn't. Still trying to warm the guy up, Ben smiled with an appreciative nod at the Devils & Dragons midway worker as the employee deposited another four goldfish SD cards into his second bulging bag with an amazing lack of enthusiasm.

The attendant—*brain-dead on his feet*—only came alive when cheers rose in the distance and he searched for what had happened.

Ben wanted to think of the guy as more than just *The Attendant*, but Cody hadn't performed anything that could possibly pass for the customary introduction. He took out his last ticket. *Crap, I totally blew my plan to only play a little each day.*

If the usual attendant, Gary, had been here, Ben would've shared his plan with him and Gary would've made sure he stuck to it. The only game Ben ever played, he had gotten to know Gary over the years and —more so now than ever—truly appreciated the man's passion for the game.

Ben shrugged at the slightly older teen with long oily hair and a scant beard that looked like he suffered from mange. Gary had kept his red, white, and black harlequin vest clean and pressed. This guy, from the looks of various stains, seemed to mainly put his uniform on when he ate.

Wishing he'd stuck to his plan, Ben extended his last ticket. "I don't understand why more people don't play this game."

"Because this game sucks." The Attendant's voice came out in harsh wheezes. As though it were Ben's fault he had the crap-job, the Attendant snatched the ticket and gave it a vicious rip. The usual red, white, and black sparkles flew from the tear. He folded a ripped half and let the other go. Like flash paper, it disappeared into a falling cascade of lights. The Attendant leaned back against the wall and used the other half of the voided coupon to scoop dark gunk from under his nails. "You're the only guy dumb—" He bit off the rest of his wheeze and peered at Ben through his oily bangs with raised eyebrows.

Ben's eyes narrowed. They both knew what the rest of the sentence would've been. His neck craned back and Ben forced his lips into a grim line. "Dumb enough to play?"

"Look," The Attendant motioned down the row,

trying to make his point. "This game is at the end of a long row of much better games."

Ben didn't turn to see. He didn't have to. He had to work his way through the throngs watching people at the seven Wrath of the Evoker booths—one more than last year—and the mass of people trying their luck at the Illusionist Shooting Galleys. Each booth on the way to the Conjurer's Course had a dwindling number of people waiting to play. With tickets in hand, a couple of younger kids had followed Ben this far only to turn back with dissatisfied groans that their curiosity hadn't paid off.

The Attendant unfolded his arm to full extension, leaned, and pointed with the ticket. "Win three times at Wrath and you get a Fireball." The Attendant spread his fingers wide. Released, the spent marker flashed away. "A flipping Fireball!" Alive for a moment, an unimpressed sneer twisted the Attendant's lips as he flopped against the wall again. "Compare that to this..." He used a limp wrist to roll his finger up the prize hierarchy in his booth. "One, goldfish. Three, cat. Nine, wolf. Twenty-seven, tuzvul. Eighty-one, treant."

As though pointing out lameness sapped his energy, the Attendant's arm went limp at his side. He motioned with his nose, barely raising his chin, as he continued. "Almost two-fifty for a minotaur and thrice that for a dragon." He then flicked Ben's first bags, brimming with goldfish spellcards. "You're good at this, man, but the best you can do is win a second treant."

Seeing the Attendant in a new light, Ben leaned away. He understood where he and the Attendant had a serious disconnect.

Since the guy worked the booth, Ben had thought they were alike. Now, he pegged this guy as exactly the type of caster he—because of Gary's annual *there's more to magic than flash-bang* lessons—despised. If he'd had this guy's narrow view of magic only being useful for combat, he wouldn't have survived his encounters at Meadows Towing.

Ben asked, "Mind telling me if you went to school around here?"

Fully materialized, the conjured frog croaked a *ribbit* to remind the player—him—that the game stood ready.

"Yeah." The Attendant leaned against the wall and watched the frog. "I did."

Ben extended his hands. Mystic reins to control the frog rose to his palms. Ben grabbed onto the invisible, leather-like strands, and he started the course. He directed the frog to make it hop only on the few yellow saucers polka dotted amongst a long field of large white plates. "Have you ever won three on Wrath?"

"Uh, yeah." The worker wheezed and chuckled as though Ben had made the understatement of the century. "More times than you could dream."

To advance, Ben released the controls when the frog landed on a small yellow plate, ending the first leg. The formerly invisible controls shimmered green when the frog vanished. Ben bent at the knees and caught the falling reins to stay in play.

A well-mannered spider monkey appeared on the left side of the game field. Ben directed the monkey to pick up darts, aim, and pitch them at a column of lavender balloons. One by one, they popped in succession up toward the violet one set at the top. Ben asked, "You ever cast a tuzvul?"

He caught a glimpse of the Attendant rolling his eyes. "More times than I care to remember."

Ben had a hard time believing that, but let it go. After all, the guy did work at a place that gave prizes away for every type of caster in the Las Vegas Valley. He could've come across one and stolen it.

With the two spare darts unused, the top balloon popped. The monkey vanished. Ben again leaned down to snatch the glimmering green controls which turned invisible in his hands.

A small air elemental pushed the pinned flaps of the top two balloons around.

Ben had the elemental form a tornado. He dipped the bottom it in the bowl of water to suck up some of the contents.

"And?" The attendant prompted.

Ben focused on the elemental. Like all conjurations, it excelled at repeating tasks. The trick? Showing it how to do it right the first time. Ben had it raise the water in the tornado, move to hover over an empty bowl and release. Guiding the tiny tornado back over to the bowl of water, he asked, "Ever cast a goldfish?"

A hard tilt bent the Attendant's neck. If his hair had been made of liquid, his bangs would have run down the side of his face. His upper lip rose and his jaw loosened, adding an exclamation point to his confusion. "Huh?"

Ben nodded at the elemental and released the reins. The controls flashed green until they hit the counter and faded. If he needed to make any changes to the commands, he'd be out of luck, but the tornado continued moving the water without further instruction.

Rummaging for the last of the red ones, Ben dug through the prize box of dusty goldfish spellcards and said, "No one ever casts goldfish."

Ben could feel the Attendant's bewilderment increase. Casters who think of magic the way the Attendant did could never see the use of casting a goldfish, and thus would never consider the container the conjuration came in as anything of value.

The first bowl had been drained and the second filled well over the top of the three red lines. Ben showed the topmost prize—four cards—to the Attendant. Sliding them into his pocket, Ben carefully lifted his prize bags.

"Duh!" The Attendant wheezed. He sneered as Ben as he began to walk away with his winnings. "Why would they?"

Ben could only shake his head at the ignorance. Recalling when Elder Komir had told him to put Jack's theft of his spellcards behind him, unresolved, he wanted to believe he would've acted differently. *If I had this many back then, I'd have done as she asked of me instead of going after the thief.* Though he seriously doubted that, he still wanted to believe it.

A man in a long Devils & Dragons red, white, and black harlequin robe walked their way from the main body of game players at the popular end of midway.

The Attendant's voice lost most of its former rasp and rose in pitch. He delivered a sing-song sentence packed with perky inflections. "Say, big winner, want to trade all those up to two treants and a cat?"

The sudden change gave Ben pause. This false, heavily-injected, excitement made him turn back. He offered the Attendant a weak smile. They both knew each other's feelings for the game. He replied with a flat, "No." Figuring the guy coming their way was probably the Attendant's supervisor, Ben wanted to wheeze out the rest. He didn't. "I like goldfish."

"So do I." The man, still beyond standard earshot, spoke out in a unique rapid cadence.

The corners of Ben's mouth shot up.

The man continued, "Their bowls, such lovely bowls, can hold such wondrous things. Things of much greater magnitude."

Ben turned. Sure enough, the robed man had a tightly cropped white beard, large ears, and a wide smile. Thin rings of varying color decorated each phalanx on both of the man's hands. Thrilled beyond measure, Ben dropped his prize bags and cheered, "Gary!"

Gary pointed to the attendant. "Please keep those in the booth for this winner, Cody." Without waiting for confirmation, Gary turned and waved for Ben to join him. "Walk with me, friend. Boy do I got a game to show you."

Chapter Six

ABOUT CASTING

AFTER SAYING 'EXCUSE ME' for the third time—without acknowledgement from the five tall Clark practitioners in their goldenrod and black lettermen's coats with hoods attached who blocked the spectator galley where Gary had told him to sit and wait—Ben lowered his shoulder and pressed through. Pushing between the last two, rapid-fire pops burst sweetened cinnamon into the air.

One of the Clark kids extended his arm. The large, coned paper cup in his hand held what remained of his order *Precious Puffs*. The bottom leaked the white icing-streaked delectable brown fluid released when a puff popped—usually in a mouth. The kid yipped, "Hey!" and lifted the bottom of the cone above his mouth and began to gulp the gooey trickle.

About to duck under the bar separating the line from the spectator gallery, a strong hand gripped Ben's shoulder. One of them hissed, "No cutsss."

Ben undid his button and with a practiced

shrugged, slipped from his coat. He dipped under the bar, and stood in the empty, three-bleacher spectator stand. "Just trying to watch."

He turned. The Clark guy holding his coat wore those contact lenses in that made his eyes look like snakes. A quick scan found the others did, too. Having a cobra as a school mascot didn't explain why they were so obsessed with looking and acting reptilian. *No one at my school acts like a gorilla.* "My coat, please."

The Clark practitioner scanned the coat's arms for a Samhain Shenanigans band. Not finding one, he tossed the trench coat on the ground, stomped on it, and kicked it to Ben's feet. Sneering to show the fanged caps over his incisors, the guy leaned on the bar and hissed, "Watch yourself. I'm venomoussss."

Ben recoiled. "And your breath's horrid."

Those nearby in the winding line chuckled.

"I know cobras don't have toothbrushes—" Ben plugged his nose. "But, *come on.*"

Most of the chuckles turned into full laughter. Near spastic with mirth, one heavy guy in a Grisham green and white three-piece suit undid his vest buttons to make room so he could double over and laugh harder.

Ben scooped his coat from the ground, slung it on, and whipped the shoulders to activate the prestidigitation. The coat rippled. Dust and dirt flew away. Something close to audacity slipped through him. While he had regretted not participating in the Shenanigans, not being in on the games gave him a certain leeway.

He moved down the row of bleachers to be at the

center for the first game at the mouth of the Devils and Dragon's midway and plopped down.

Having squeezed through the crowds earlier to get to his favorite game with the seemingly living-dead attendant, Cody, Ben had assumed this game was another *Wrath of the Evoker*. It had the same thirty-foot-glasssteel-cube-seperating-two-ten-foot-glassteel-cubes set up. Except where the competitor's cubes in Wrath were darkly-tented, both of these remained as clear as the large one separating them.

If I would've turned my head, instead of heading right to the Conjurer's Challenge, *I'd seen the ghostly six-feet tall* Challenge the Conjurer 500 *booth title forming from, and dissolving into, ambient emerald energy. I only had to glance.*

Gary stepped into the right-hand cube and raised his hands to the crowd.

Someone called, "He's back!"

A round of applause erupted from the casters in line.

Forgetting to hiss, the self-proclaimed venomous boy yelled, "You're going down, Gary. I'm going to become the new House Champion."

Ben counted eight people ahead of the Clark guy as Gary scanned the line.

"We'll find out in eight minutes, son." Gary gave his bearded cheek one long, slow stroke, and smiled. "With your schoolmates helping, you might have a chance."

Gary shot Ben a thumbs-up.

Ben returned it.

Gary rolled back his red, white, and black harlequin sleeves and nodded to a similarly dressed redhead orchestrating the ticket collection. Small jeweled earrings ran the curve of her large ears.

Figuring each jewel was a spell focus, and not knowing of a school that used earrings, Ben wondered under his breath, "Where'd she learned to cast?"

"Sssay," the venomous boy hissed, "Trencher?"

"What?" Ben answered, but didn't turn. His focus went from the ticket-taker's ear to the four large amethysts on her plump cheek. He couldn't quite tell if they were embedded or in piercings.

"You know that guy? The House Champ?"

Though it was a lie, Ben shook his head. If he spent time talking to the Clark Cobra, he'd miss out on watching Gary.

A voice, feminine and high-pitched, said, "I do. He's a ring-caster."

Ben tried to see the speaker, but from where he sat he could only see the people at the front of the winding line and legs.

"So is his daughter," she added.

Ben's gaze went back to the redhead. He studied her profile and could see Gary's pronounced brow in her features.

"He taught at Charon's Chantry in St. Louis years ago, before it shutdown. Heard he was three down from the School Master there."

Ben had spent a lot of time with Gary through the various Samhain Festivals. While the woman had been mostly right, Gary had been the school's Master Conjurer—*only two down from the Master*—before the school closed six years ago. Tempted to correct the woman, Ben kept his mouth shut.

Since learning of conjuration and meeting Gary during his first Samhain Festival, Ben had checked around and found none of the schools in the Las Vegas Valley taught the conjuration. When he had asked, Gary attributed the decline to the top-tier competitors of the Spell Dueling Sport League opting for the crowd-pleasing flash-bang of Evocation.

As if on cue, there was a series of *pops* and astonished *oohs* from behind him. Ben didn't take his focus from Gary's booth.

The first competitor—a Dunn-Blatt with his hood up—stepped in and his cube darkened. A glowing red counter, set at twenty-five, appeared on both Gary's cube and the challenger's. The shifting *Challenge the Conjuror 500*, title became *501*.

Ben's jaw unhinged. The 'five hundred' he'd thought was part of the game title turned out to be the growing pool for beating Gary. Recalling the mundane wanting to buy his seventy-two tickets, Ben equated the prize to more than his mystically aware—but mundane—father, a dealer at a prestigious casino, made in a year. He whispered, "Well, that explains the line." Not sure he could beat Gary, the reward still made him want to try. "Good thing I don't have any more tickets," he murmured.

A bolt of violet energy flew from the dark square, across the center, and crashed against the wall before Gary. The twenty-five on Gary's cube dropped to twenty-four.

Though a phantom fight, Ben's pulse lurched and he fought the urge to cast at the challenger to help Gary.

Gary twisted a ring on his thumb. A vibrant orange German Shepherd appeared in the center of the cube and charged.

Another violet bolt from the Dunn-Blatt's cube dropped Gary's meter another point.

The energy faded from the dog as it became as deadly as any real dog for the spell's duration. Gary twisted a ring on his other hand and a teal hummingbird fluttered close to him in the center cube.

The dog attacked the Dunn-Blatt's glass.

The challenger's meter dropped by a point.

Another violet bolt flew from the challenger's cube.

The hummingbird, still glowing with greenish-blue magic, intercepted the blast and dispersed it. Dimmer—but still present—the teal bird hovered in place.

Gary twisted his dog ring again. Another dog, a Doberman Pinscher this time, appeared next to the German Shepherd.

The challenger's counter ticked down by two.

Gary remained focused on whatever he saw in the dark cube, but didn't cast again. Occasionally, he shot the hummingbird forward to deflect a different evocation, but the man Ben had learned conjuration from seemed as relaxed as though he were the conductor of a train moving down the rails to a foregone final stop to let this guy off and hurry the next rider on.

Under a minute later, the Dunn-Blatt caster burst from the dark cube. The darkened glass returned to being completely clear again. Ben stood to watch the hooded caster. Eagerly, he rushed to the end of the line.

The ticket taker extended her hand to an adult in yellow robes who handed over two tickets. She slid one into a slot next to the cube; the clear door opened. The man in yellow slid his sleeves back as he stepped in and the cube darkened again.

This time, Ben saw Gary's daughter put the second ticket into a different slot. The prize counter ticked up.

Even though the guy in yellow solely threw fireballs, the match pretty much went the same way, except for Gary using lions and an eagle instead of dogs and a hummingbird.

The count kept building as player after player entered, played, and lost. The game line kept growing.

No one could beat Gary.

Enthralled Ben almost lost track of time. Though his main objective for coming to the festival had been to win as many obdurium enhanced goldfish SD cards, so he could overwrite them with other spells, Crystal—a girl he considered to be his own personal seer—would kick his butt if he didn't see the diviner she idolized. *Diviners' Row will be the first part of the festival to close, but the education from watching Gary dominate is too much of a gift to turn away from.* Though Crystal had said she had to ask Papa Mojo for a personal favor to give Ben a reading, Ben chose to stay, and focus on trying to understand the 'why' behind when Gary would change tactics.

The dark cube became transparent again and the man in the yellow robes, who had lost early and had made the line again, beamed a tenacious grin and asked in an anxious squeak, "Right, so?"

Ben frowned. *Right, so what? You lost, buddy. You get back in line, again. That's what.*

Speaking in his fast patter, Gary gave his cropped beard that slow—*class is in session*—stroke Ben loved to see. "You've ramped up to a more powerful spell, but fared no better than your first two goes." Gary spread his fingers, tapped the index, the middle, and gripped his ring finger. "Think. Other than using conjuration, evocation, or more powerful evocation, you've done the same thing each time." Gary let go of his hand and motioned at the man in yellow as though he were trying to pull and answer from his reluctant mouth.

"I—" The guy paused and slapped his forehead. "I'm only casting one spell."

Gary clapped once, hard, and pointed at the man as though driving a nail home with one hammer-blow.

A jealous twinge cramped Ben's stomach and then rolled through. For a moment, he felt betrayed that Gary wasn't exclusively sharing his knowledge with only him. Then, he came to his senses. Gary had the kind of knowledge that shouldn't be kept locked away. *If only Senior Adept Collins was here to learn this higher lesson.*

Upon thinking the Senior Adept's name, a sneer turned Ben's lips. He wanted to spit. *Why'd that blonde bastard pop into my head?* To clear the building contempt for, arguably, the APA's most despised instructor, Ben wiped his forehead and flicked his hand as though he were throwing off sweat. *I'm not going to let the simple thought of Collins ruin the evening.*

Re-focused, he returned to watching Gary kick butt. Class was in session.

THE VENDOR CARTS of the Fae Fort Food Court were in full swing. Ben's eyes kept darting to Southern Sweets with their oversized red, white, and blue-striped umbrella. With a burning desire, he tortured his stomach by watching the workers spin cotton candy, inflate Precious Puffs, and load the soon-to-be aromatic festival popcorn kernels into a second deep kettle popper.

Gary had offered to get him something, but—to keep from feeling like a mooch—Ben had declined.

If he'd stuck with this plan—if he hadn't gotten caught up trying to show Cody, the oily-haired-undead-attendant how cool the game he worked was—Ben could've used a ticket—*just one*—to get a dine-all-night wristband and, as Gary dug into his gooey, chopped bacon-laden cheese shells, Ben could've been munching on the popcorn he'd been fiending for.

At Gary's request, Ben rattled on about his school year and his dislike for Senior Adept Collins strictly academic. As he recapped the year, Gary, the six hundred-streak strong and still undefeated House Champ of *Challenge the Conjurer*, shoveled food during his break.

Someone in an Archon Private Academy trench coat sauntered through the food court. More from the hell-with-all swagger than the spikey blonde flat-top, Ben recognized Collins. He slumped in his chair to use Gary, who sat across the table from him, as a shield to keep Collins from seeing him. "Man, how does he do it?"

Between spoonfuls, Gary glanced over his shoulder, returned to eating, and asked, "Who do what?"

"Collins." Ben pointed. "The A. P. A. guy."

Gary didn't turn. "What'd he do?"

"Nothing." Struggling to put his finger on exactly what it was, Ben shrugged. "I mean, I don't know. It just seems as though whenever I think about him, he appears."

Mid-route to his mouth, Gary's hand stopped. Tiny bacon chunks dangled in the strings of cheese between fork and plate like flies in a spider web.

Moving toward the chain-link fence between the food court and the employees only area, Collins' demeanor changed slightly to being watchful.

Ben could feel Gary's appraising stare, but kept his eyes on Collins as he walked to the fence and began to look around. Ben sunk down further.

Gary asked, "Is this normal?"

"Me hiding?" Squinting, Ben considered it.

Collins eyes landed on someone and he gave a courtly acknowledgement nod.

Ben didn't check to see who. "Well—" There had to

be a reason why Collins was acting suspiciously, and Ben wasn't going to let the Senior Adept out of his sight. "He doesn't like me and has made trouble for me." About to spill his adventure with Penelope, Ben made a quick conversational turn back to school. "If my spells are one line of code longer than they're supposed to be, he gives me a zero."

"That's not what I mean." Gary's fork thudded on the paper plate.

Ben adjusted to the right. Instead of being a shield, Gary seemed to be leaning into Ben's line of sight. Almost like a weird, slow dance, Ben kept leaning further than Gary, and Gary leaned to make eye contact.

Without eye contact, Gary asked, "Is it normal for you to think of people and then they show?"

"No." Ben shifted directions to peek around Gary's other side. Dominic, Collins' favorite student, who couldn't get even a simple cantrip programmed in less than a thousand lines, walked up to the Senior Adept. Collins went rigid at being approached. He gave a thin smile and shook Dominic's hand. Ben answered, "It started happening about a month ago."

Gary said, "Ben." And waited for his attention.

Ben remained focused on Collins. The Senior Adept seemed to be struggling to get Dominic to go away. Seeing the blond jerk put out by a coddled student brought a pleased smile to Ben's mouth. *Almost serves him right.* The area around Collins and Dominic dimmed slightly before, woodenly, Dominic turned and walked away.

Gary raised a finger in front of Ben's face. "Attention."

Ben shook his head and sat up in his chair to peer over Gary's white hair as Dominic—*Dom's legs are lightning rod stiff*—walked away. "Hold on. I think Collins is up to something."

A handclap preceded a glowing green stone wall, eight feet tall and wide, materialized behind Gary. No amount of leaning would allow Ben to see Collins. After a moment, the glow faded leaving a gray, freestanding wall.

About to get up, Ben turned to admonish Gary with an annoyed glance, but his eyes went to a rocking stopwatch Gary had out. Ben's eyes locked onto the timepiece as it moved side to side in graceful, captivating arcs.

More than he desired festival food, Ben desperately wanted to observe Collins, but he couldn't pull his attention away from the steady *tick* of the thin steel second hand which became the center of his existence. In five seconds Ben felt his consciousness swinging side to side with the watch, like the phantom pull of waves after being in the ocean all day, as he became dislodged from the present and forced into the timepiece.

The continuous hum of the fairgrounds dimmed, replaced by the constant, reliable *ticks* and perfect seconds of silence. The thick aromas faded and were overtaken with a sterile, metallic tang. A white fog filled his eyes, washing the bustle of the food court away into the pure white of the stopwatch's face, with black frets at fixed points in his peripheral vision.

The second hand stopped, yet the timepiece's ticking—steady, constant, precise—continued.

Gary's voice, amplified and inescapable, boomed, "I

apologize for this inconvenience, my friend, but I need your complete attention for just a minute. Heed me, Ben. Underground duels are extremely dangerous. You may have won, and could continue winning, but only the worst sort of people go there to wager on the outcome. Win too often, and the people who lost too much betting on you to lose will come after you. Lose too often, and those who bet too much on you to win will try to kill you. While you may gain abilities, like this third-eye of yours, the risk is not worth it. Heed me, Ben. Wait until you're eighteen and can legally join the dueling circuits. Heed me, Ben, and I will help you."

In an instant, the second hand swung around. The stopwatch face—which had been lain over everything and had become everything—burst like a water balloon.

The glorious spectacle of the Samhain Festival washed back over Ben. Momentarily aware of his heightened sense of things, reality inundated Ben's fading amplified cognizance and brought him to safe rest at a table across from Gary where he could see lights strung between tents, hear the bark of street performers, smell the perfume of festival popcorn, and feel the growing hunger in his gut.

Ben found his head rotating. Unconsciously, he tried to keep up with the stopwatch as Gary spun it on a chain around his index finger.

His head wound tightening circles until Gary caught the timepiece.

As though waking up, Ben blinked. He dug his pinkies into his ears to clear what remained of the focused silence. *Had a minute passed?* If so, his memory of it began to fade... Until he focused.

Something he hadn't known about, hadn't been aware of, kept the unreal pocket watch—*time bubble*—reality intact. "Underground duels?" Vaguely remembering that he was trying to observe something or someone, Ben stood because it felt like what he had been wanting to do. He walked to the wall. "Didn't know they existed." He peeked around the edge and spied Collins scowling after a retreating A. P. A. student. Ben wondered who, but had recaptured his razor-sharp focus on the suspicious Senior Adept. A strong grip landed on Ben's shoulder and spun him.

With surprising strength, Gary had physically turned him to get—and got—that probing eye contact everyone over twenty seemed to possess. "You have battled someone, have you not?"

Ben had learned how to keep secrets when pinned by the stare. He hadn't expected it from Gary which made him slow in clamping his eyes shut and—before he could lock them away—Ben failed at not recalling the sense of betrayal as Jack ran away with his spellcards, and the near-choking fear he felt as the Krotosian ogre hurled blasts at him.

Gary gripped harder and shook. "That's not how this works."

Ben turned his face away, closed his eyes tighter, and consciously placed the two thoughts in a thick, solid-steel mental cube.

Gary's voice took on an anxious tone as he stated, "You *have* battled." Gary grabbed Ben's other shoulder and tried to regain eye contact. "Don't hide this from me, Ben. I'm trying to help."

This is Gary, Ben. Drawing a deep breath, Ben

exhaled, opened his eyes, and slowly lowered his defenses to the one adult he considered to be a friend.

"This lesser oracular ability," Gary started, "You won it from someone named—" Ben's memory of the build up to duel at the Suntouched Stronghold's stables opened for Gary to analyze. That moment when Jack turned to face Ben to battle froze. Though Ben had been focused on Jack's face, Gary worked at the edges of the moment. The master conjurer's arms went limp. His eyes flew wide, and his voice dropped low in astonishment. "You've been to the other side..."

Gary began to roll the memory forward.

Ben blinked hard and shut Gary out. He had to, otherwise his mentor would see him activating a Nilosian-tainted Heracles enchantment. *If Gary has a chance to see that, he'll doubtlessly lock onto it.*

The urge to run overtook Ben. To keep his Nilosian secret, he had to get away.

Gary's arms went to grab his shoulders.

Ben dodged, pivoted, and sprung away.

Gary whispered after him. "Let me finish."

Chapter Eight

SENIOR ADEPT COLLINS

BEN WENT around the edge of Gary's wall and hurried to get in line at Southern Sweets. He still didn't have a way to pay, but being in line got him away from Gary and, more importantly, to a place where he could see Collins more clearly.

To not stand out as an APA student, he took off his coat, folded it, and held it over his belt buckle. The fresh batch of popcorn started to pop and flow over the edge of the kettle. For a moment, he looked away from Collins to longingly eye the bin pooling with the hot, butter-laced goodness. *If I only had a bag to dive into.* A slight gust, meant to fan the smells through the fairground blew through the line. He wasn't alone in inhaling the smorgasbord of treats, nor was his stomach alone in growling.

Unable to take the torturous scents any longer, Ben hustled to the middle ring of the food court to post up near the series of large manila spiced cider tents.

Collins' hands worked the air. The Senior Adept

didn't touch the tablet on his hip and he didn't have a spellcard in hand. Collins' hands simply moved in circles before an Argosian-red bubble surrounded him.

Not seeing any of the other methods of casting around Collins, Ben wondered, "How is he casting?" He'd only seen people cast empty-handed on the other side, when he met Elder Komir. She—and the others— made the point that he wasn't a wizard awfully clear. A nearly undetectable disdain clung to their words, and Bo, the bouncer, had threatened him for clinging to the idea of being a wizard.

The magic bubble around Collins burst, coating the Senior Adept with red mystic mist, giving his blond hair an orange glow. Recognizing part of the effect, Ben identified the spell. "Non-Detection." His shoulder rose in a non-impressed half shrug. While not common, most wouldn't care to learn it since all the spell did was ensure that the caster would not be preternaturally observed casting other spells, Non-Detection lay just beyond Ben's own casting ability—he would be learning it the next couple of years, when he became a full Apprentice. "Not bad."

Refusing to believe Collins capable of being a real wizard, Ben scrutinized the Senior Adept to find the alternate method of casting. From the corner of his eye, he noticed Gary come around the wall, looking for him.

Collins faced the fence.

Ben changed location again, trying to mask his hurry with a careful speed-walk as he weaved through the dense crowds strolling amid full dining tables at the center of the food court.

He glanced back to see if anyone had started to take

notice of him, and discovered Gary, still standing near the wall he'd made, motioning for Ben to return.

No way. Ben shook his head.

Gary sighed and, heading back toward the direction of the *Challenge the Conjurer* booth, walked away.

Ben neared the other spiced cider tents closer to Collins and focused on the man again.

Again, the Senior Adept pulled another spell from the air around him.

Ben frowned. He had missed what conjuring tool Collins had used and there wasn't anything obvious about the somatic aspect of the spell he had cast.

Collins hunkered down into a squat and then leapt. He cleared the twenty-foot chain-link fence and landed on the other side. There, Collins waved his hand over his face and stood photograph still.

In a whirl of gray robes, four Primaries appeared on the Employees Only side of the fence around Collins. The tip of their battle rods lit. Seemingly ready, red energy pulsed along their length, obscuring their hands in Argosian magic. Scowling, each scanned the area totally oblivious to Collins, standing right in their midst.

A Vibrosian Magistrate—the one from the parking lot—appeared in a whirl of robes. She glanced around.

The Argosians shook their heads at her.

She lifted her weapon into the air and squeezed it. The baton pulsed orange and sent a rippling wave of energy out in a thirty-foot radius. Some clinging to the air where Collins had leapt from the food court, most of it faded.

Bopping their batons first, all five Magistrates

twirled their robes and were gone. Three swirls flashed on the food court side of the fence. The Vibrosian and two Argosians appeared next to the Vibrosian glow highlight where Collins had been moments before. The other two Argosian Magistrates did not reappear.

Directly behind the Primaries, Collins began to walk backward and then turned away, to jog further into the employee area.

A devious smile crooked the corners of Ben's mouth as he realized the amazing spell he grossly misidentified as Non-Detection proved to be a much stronger one. In spite of extreme dislike for the Senior Adept, Ben couldn't keep the awe from his voice. "He knows Obfuscation."

Watching Collins move further away from the Magistrates, Ben wished he knew if the spell was a seven, eight, or nine-stone spell. Whatever level, the Archon Private Academy—or any school he knew of— didn't teach anything from those lofty tiers. While no one would say as much, there seemed to be a general rule against it.

The Vibrosian and an Argosian Magistrates whirled their robes and disappeared. The other Argosian, a short squat man, strode into the food court, scooped a bratwurst, then twirled his robes and disappeared as well.

Collins faded into the darkness obscuring the festival's employee area.

"Damn it!" Ben rushed through the crowd. A long string of apologies spilled from his mouth as he bumped the rest of his way through the busier parts of the Fae Fort Food Court.

Finally next to the gate, Ben checked behind him. There were a few people who had waited for him to look their way so they could shoot him dirty looks, but no one stayed focused on him.

Ben pulled the large, silver, anti-divination ring he had earned at Meadows Towing. Like the belt around his waist that had also been sized for an ogre, and shrunk to fit him, Ben poked his thumb into the wide band. Keeping the same ratios, the ring shrank to a snug fit. A wave of warm magic flowed through his core. *Wonder if I just flashed with magic.*

An orc's gruff voice—*no lilted vowels, so it's not Toad*—came from the ring: "Might-Fist, return to Meadows Towing." *All the other orcs pretty much all sound the same.*

Ben extended his arm and considered the ring to see if he could see the message on it. *No.* Being the Might-Fist, Ben felt obligated to return if they needed help. *But they didn't actually call for help. Last time they wanted me, they wanted me to pick out which color t-shirts they were going to get the Meadows Towing logo silkscreened on.*

Collins momentarily came back from the darkness, turning to go a different direction in the fenced area.

Ben pulled out his Anvilsmith. If the matter with the orcs proved to be really important, they'd leave a better message. *Or, maybe, actually use the landline I had installed at Meadows Towing to actually call my tablet.*

He eyed the top of the fence to consider how much power to put into his leap. Thinking on what he planned on doing, his head shook in disbelief. Employees Only at the Samhain Festival meant *employees only*. Unlike trying to sneak into Pepperjacks, he'd just seen Primaries show up in force.

Ben didn't know the penalty for crossing into the employee area, but Collins was up to something and he had to give chase. If he were caught and had a chance to point or speak, he would try his best to implicate Collins.

From casting hundreds of spells through the years, Ben's fingers slid over his Anvilsmith tablet without him needing to look. Lighting first on *Spells*, his finger tapped where the asterisk for his *Enchantment* spells would populate, and he tapped the spot where the icon for *Leap* would be.

Still waking, the screen flashed twice and the tarsier leaping from a branch background populated along with the *Cast* button made to look like a tarsier's bugged eyes. He tapped *Cast*.

Since earlier in the month, he had gotten used to the slight vibration from his device flowing magic into him instead of forcing it. Ben had even got used to faking being shocked when forced to cast at school. However, *Leap* only costing one arcane watt which still seemed weird.

Aiming for where Collins had landed, Ben crouched, leapt over the chain-link fence, and landed exactly where Collins had on the employee's side.

Fear tightened his muscles. Not visible from the other side of the fence, he had jumped into the middle of five—four red, one orange—rotating scrying sensors. All bobbed in the air above weird symbols like the ones he had seen in the Arcane Alehouse.

Worse yet, his gaze fell directly into the sensor left by the Vibrosian.

He clamped his eyes shut and he braced for impact.

Chapter Nine

TRESPASSING

BEN HAD HEARD rumors of the Magistrates being brutal, but he hadn't believed it until he saw the way the four Argosians teleported in ready to throw down. He had been outclassed—*mystically dwarfed, really*—at the Arcane Alehouse. Unlike like then, it might take the Primaries a bit to realize he wasn't fighting back.

A sudden coolness—*wind? A spell?*—on his flesh set Ben's pulse racing. Blood thumped in his empty stomach and sang in his ears. As prepared for a beating as he could be, Ben pointed in the direction Collins had gone.

What would Master Reynolds think?

A small burst of air escaped him. Then he laughed more fully before stifling it.

It struck him funny that he cared more about what Master Reynolds' reaction would be than that of his parents, but it made sense. Being brought before anyone for wrongdoing by the Magistrates meant receiving the worst allowable punishment. While his parents could ground him—indefinitely—Master Reynolds would expel him. With no other technomancy schools in southern Nevada, it would effectively end Ben's mystical education.

Though his magical career options would be extremely limited, a sudden wistfulness overtook him. *Maybe when I turn twenty-five—and, perhaps, no longer grounded—I could work the Conjuration Course. The booth doesn't need a caster near Gary's skill level, but it deserves someone a great deal better than Cody.*

Ready to explain, he opened his eyes.

The five eyeball sensors still scanned the area. Undisturbed, the symbols under each gracefully bobbed up and down. The mark under the orange one looked identical to the glowing glyph on the tip of the Vibrosian Primary's baton. It also looked like one of the symbols from the book Elder Komir had given him.

The darkness, which had obscured the employee area on the other side of the fence, began to blow away like someone had turned on a high-powered fan and the shadows were simply dense smoke leaving the area brightly lit by lights atop the scores of industrial shipping containers and double, or triple-hauled semi-trailers. Long corridors formed between the two mass shipping options.

Ben released his breath. Breathing a bit easier, the aroma of Bugsy's Brats swam around him and, now, he understood why the short Primary had grabbed one.

In case gestures were important, Ben repeated what Collins' had done. He bent down, twisted to avoid the sensors, walked backwards, then turned to jog the way Collins had gone.

Since the Senior Adept was neither directly ahead nor in sight at the first intersection. Ben occasionally squatted to scan as far as he could see under the truck trailers. Even though he knew both the starwise and mundane parts of the festival were in full swing, the absence of anyone in the employees' area bothered him. When he ducked down, he kept excepting to come eye-to-eye with a guard dog or an attack boar, but—thankfully—never did.

Starting to huff from the squats, Ben spied movement a few rows up and several columns over; where the long trailers and shipping containers gave way to smaller trucks, cars, and crates. He stayed low long enough to distinguish the swish of a trench coat before sprinting down the corridor.

He put his coat back on and peered around the corner.

Collins entered a dark, old-fashioned, old-west type stagecoach wagon. Leaving the windows open, thin pink hands, with slim fingers, closed the shades inside on which shadows, cast by candlelight, danced.

Not certain if the ring masked his sounds, Ben kept his suspicion unspoken. *Bet it's the woman with the elfy-ears that Collins had dinner with last month.*

Staying vigilant for employees, Ben crept closer to the antique wagon to eavesdrop. Even at two in the morning, the carnival still went on strong and no one else walked amongst the wagons. This would change in an hour or so when the mundanes petered away.

Strong sizzling—*black magic?*—sounds rose as he neared the wagon. *What kind of Nilosian spells are they silently casting in there?* Then the scent of sausage and peppers came through the window.

"Well, my love—" Speaking Elven, the woman's light voice carried the majestic, airy intonations better than Adept Yeffaux, the Archon Private Academy's Master Linguist. "How did it go?"

"Better than could be expected," Collins gruff voice replied in Elven. The Senior Adept often claimed he did not know the language, but obviously—by his proper inflection of the vowels—that was a complete lie. "Better than could be expected." Glass clinked. Silence filled the next few seconds. Collins continued, "He took Grand in two categories and got an Ad Hoc bonus."

"Amazing," She cooed.

Collins agreed, "I know."

Ben's jaw dropped and his mouth began to dry. He was the only magic faire entrant awarded a bonus this year. Why were they talking about him? Motion in the distance caught his attention. Keeping his ears perked, Ben turned to evaluate the movement.

Along the length of the distant fence separating the employees only area from the starwise parking, ran two girls in white shirts.

Ben strained to see what color their skirts were, but it was too dark and too far to be sure.

The woman asked, "Think I can approach him early?"

"No," Collins barked. "The path has been set..."

Three wisps of green energy—*tethers*—shot at the girls. The lines missed and the girls turned away from the fence to run into the packed parking lot.

Hooded figures—*Clark? Dunn-Blatt?*—gave chase.

"You..." Collins continued

The woman giggled.

Collins continued, "Must be patient and walk it."

The emerald lines of energy flashed repeatedly from the aggressors toward the white-shirted girls. One of the lines went tight. A long, terrified scream full of desperate fright rocketed their way.

The scream gave Ben goose bumps

Even from so far away, the shriek had been belted fiercely enough to be heard halfway through the employee lot, but the cry would be battled back and swallowed by the mirth from the fairground.

The wagon shook a little. The woman asked, "Should you go check on that, my love?"

Beyond, near the girls, a bright flash of orange blossomed as a tall woman—*no, a centaur, the Sunrise Mountain Sisterhood summon centaurs*—materialized. The first row of distant cars blocked the legs, but most of the horse-like body stood taller than the hoods. Green flashed next to the orange, and another centaur formed.

Collins' sniggered. It held a *you should know better* sound. "That was a girl."

Near the aggressors, emerald flashes flanked the violet glow of Krotosian energy.

Another scream rolled across the lot.

Collins gave another dirty chuckle, and added, "I work at an all-boys school, remember?"

Ben couldn't see what the deep purple energy formed, but the two greens each summoned dangerous dusk buffaloes; the four thick prehensile tendrils on each beasts' back were reared up. Dunn-Blatts. Since discovering Malcolm had become a Dunn-Blatt after being booted from the APA, an instant dislike of the school—and its attendees—had taken root in Ben.

An elastic band snapped against flesh. The woman gave a slight yelp. Collins chuckled. "So, it's no one I'm responsible for."

A second snap sounded. The woman gave off something close to a whimper. "What if one of your boys caused it?"

Collins's constantly annoyed tone fell away and the Senior Adept's voice took on a never-heard-before warmth. "If it's my boys, let them have their fun. After all, it's Samhain."

Low and throaty, the woman replied, "Mmm-hmm."

Not a single Samhain Festival had gone by without reports of horrible things happening. What seemed to be taking place out in the starwise lot could be one of those dreadful rumors. Ben knew it. Collins knew it. In fact, the Senior Adept had implied one of the worst acts, and had no qualms about letting it happen.

Wishing he had a way to set part of the wagon on fire, Ben stood, scowled at it, and started toward the parking lot.

Chapter Ten

PART OF THE SOLUTION

NOT FOR THE FIRST TIME, Ben thought about programming spells directly to his Anvilsmith tablet's quick-launch bar. When he had tried in the past, the tablet wouldn't let the spells be assigned to the bottom row. Other Archon Private Academy students had unlocked their devices to install some cool cosmetic hacks, but he'd seen nothing substantial from a functionality point of view.

Unable to afford a replacement if he happened to brick his device, Ben had been afraid to hack his. The potential ridicule for showing up to *Spell Programming IIX* with his brightly painted, five-year-old Rainbow tablet proved enough to keep him from trying, but— Seeing Senior Adept and the lady together again— brought to mind the spare Anvilsmith tablet, deep in his closet. With the device came an old unanswered question. *Why had Collins switch a cursed device for my perfectly good one?*

Ben put the question out of his mind. He hadn't

figured it out before, and thinking about it now only made him angry again. Instead, as his fingertips worked the cool glass on his tablet to enter his passcode, he focused on helping the girls. *Well, at least evening the odds.*

He tapped the fat exclamation point and, for the first time, noticed the slight wait for the icons of his seven *Conjurations* spells to populate. There had always been a lag. However, compared to the near-instant speed of casting from spellcards, these multiple one-second-between taps could add up to that *difference between life and death* Adept Love continually spouted during the *Dueling* classes.

Ben came to a stop. Instead of waiting for the various screens to populate, he mentally placed the locations he needed to tap in his head. After his tap of the lightning bolt icon for *Usain,* his speed spell, he sped through the rest of his taps.

He tapped where *Cast* would populate, swiped back up to *Conjurations*, tapped where the kangaroo icon would be for his *Tarsier Leap* spell, and tapped where the *Cast* button would be.

The splash screen showing Usain Bolt running through a finished line ribbon, arms raised in a 'vee,' appeared. The highly italicized *Cast* button lit. Energy vibrated into him and his mouth filled with the taste of oranges. The *Usain* spell screen swiped away. The kangaroo icon lit, and the Tarsier in a tree background shown.

Not waiting for the *Cast* button to depress, Ben smiled at his ingenuity and started running toward the parking lot. The wagons and trailers he ran past turned into flashes, the wind whipped at his hair and flapped his trench coat. The Anvilsmith vibrated again and magic thrummed in his legs.

His strides lengthened.

His speed increased further.

Coming up fast on the chain-link fence, Ben leapt to keep from ramming into it.

He cleared the fence, the confrontation, and eight rows of parked cars.

As he sailed over, a burst of green magic flashed as a centaur, having been ravaged by two dusk buffaloes, winked from existence. The triumphant beasts became indistinguishable from the dark lot, but their growls surrounded the two girls on the lone centaur's back. The three Dunn-Blatt boys were toying with them, savoring the pending victory.

Ben landed between aisles and slid into a pickup truck. The pause ended the speed spell, stealing the delicious orange taste from his rapidly drying mouth.

He wanted to channel Argosian into his Orion spell card to handle the dusk buffaloes, and Dunn-Blatts, but remembered all-too-well Oscar and Abe slaying half the orcs.

Bastion has awakened at the promise of combat, and offered the Nilosian energy.

Ben refused to use it. More worrisome than the disgusting cracks that had sounded from Jack's arm breaking between jagged Nilosian teeth, was the energy's way of not doing what he willed of it.

Hoping to be in time, Ben began to sneak between cars back toward the confrontation.

Keeping an eye on the girls—*they're the same Sunrise*

Mountain girls from when I arrived tonight—and their centaur, he ran his fingers along his spellcard holder until he felt the three grooves indicating his fingertip had lit on Orion. Anvilsmith in the other hand, Ben focused on feeling for the energy inside his device.

One of the boys spoke to the girls in a factual, articulated way. "Did you know that three casters die each night of the Shenanigans? It's true, look it up."

Was that true? Ben had kept track of the various facts that he'd learned about the Shenanigans through the years, and though he had seen injuries, he hadn't heard about any fatalities.

The arcane wattage within his device answered his call. A smile spread across Ben's lips as the warm, green power thrummed from this device, through him, and into the Orion spellcard. Peeking through car windows, Ben summoned an emerald gorilla to each of the five points of a star behind cars around the boys. To not steal the girls' fight, he only planned on using one at a time, but—since the boys were talking about death— Ben had the other four at the ready.

"They won't be able to," voice husky from laughing, another boy added. "But at least there will only be one other death tonight."

"Didn't your teachers tell you to stay on the fairgrounds?" Ben searched out who said that. The three boys kept their mystic shadows obscuring their faces in their hoods, but he'd know that voice anywhere. It was Malcolm. "So, what are you girls willing to give up to keep living?"

The same height as the other tall Dunn-Blatt, Ben spied Malcolm by the cocky way he stood. Refusing to let the jerk have the upper hand one second longer, Ben had his gorillas hop from their hiding spots and attack the dusk buffaloes.

"Apes!" the first boy called.

Two gorillas landed on each of the green dusk buffaloes. One charged forward to challenge Malcolm's purple conjuration and—programmed to fight intelligently—paused when the wild beast spun and roared.

"Hook them!" Trying to locate the casters, Malcolm scanned the parking lot. "Commit them to a challenge!"

"There's five of them!" The husky-voiced one turned and ran as one of the dusk buffaloes fell beneath two gorillas. "Run!"

Given how easily his gorillas passed the green beasts' tendrils, the monsters couldn't have been *true* dusk buffaloes. The *Mythic Monster I* course had explained how deadly the creatures were. *The greens must just be regular buffaloes designed to look the part.*

The other boy gave a fist pump when his conjuration gored the throat away from one of the gorillas, but he released his hook and ran when another gorilla broke his beast's neck.

Malcolm stood alone, turning, and searching to find the gorillas' casters. His, probably real, purpled-eyed beast stared hard at the centaur, though it backed toward its caster when the gorillas began to encircle it.

The girls climbed from the orange centaur's back. The long haired, tie-less one produced a stone arrow tip from her coat pocket, and flicked her wrist at Malcolm. An emerald tether shot out and hooked into Malcolm's eye. Unfortunately, unable to do physical damage, the hook shifted to his chest.

"Come out of hiding, cowards!" Malcolm threw his head back and bellowed, "Line up, apes! I'll take each of you on!"

Ben stood from where he crouched and walked out into the lane. "Fight her first." He ground his fist into his palm. "Then we'll know if we have to turn you into a statistic."

Malcolm sneered. "I should have known that you, and your chicken-shit friends, couldn't face me like a men."

Don't be goaded into something stupid. Ben rubbed his chin. He tried to muster a lazy grin to mimic Malcolm's earlier smug smile. "We're just using the tactics you and your boys taught us."

Out of nowhere—*no, from my ring*—an orc's gruff voice called, "Please return to Meadows Towing."

Ben stiffened.

Neither Malcolm nor the girls reacted.

They didn't hear the orc's loud and clear request. Interesting.

With a pissed flick of his wrist, Malcolm dismissed his dusk buffalo. He pulled his hood and the shadow magic that had obscured his face splashed away. Defiant in relenting, he looked at the girl who had hooked him. "What do you want?"

She said, "Your tie." Her icy stare said, *your life.*

Sneering, Malcolm removed it and dropped it on the ground. The girl released her hook, and he turned to leave.

"Not so fast." Ben dismissed one of the gorillas and

had the remaining three crouch to be ready to attack. As much as he wanted to turn them loose to beat down the Dunn-Blatt, it wouldn't have been right and Malcolm—being Malcolm—probably wouldn't learn anything from it. *No, I gotta do something that would bother, but not harm, him.*

The Dunn-Blatt turned back to face him.

Locking eye contact, Ben walked to Malcolm, his hand extended between them. "I'll take your hook."

Chapter Eleven

A CASUAL INSULT

STILL AMAZED that Malcolm had the tool that had been used to rip him into the horrible reality of dueling in his hand, Ben rubbed the rusty nail which had served as Malcolm's focus. Besides the rough surface, there was nothing special about it. However, on this cool autumn night, heavy with the sounds and fragrances of the festival, the nail—now, through cultural tradition, Ben's possession—meant more in victory than his wins at the Magic Faire.

One of the girls cleared her throat

Ben turned.

They gave their courtly introductions and names with curtsies. The tieless brunette. "Sarah Coleman."

The pixie-cut blonde. "Clarissa Twinstar."

Though Ben wanted to break free and return to the dark wagon where Collins and the woman talked about him, re-entering the employees only area with anyone watching was out of the question. Ben bowed deeply, introduced himself. "Benjamin Baxter. And we should get moving before the Dunn-Blatts return with most of their school in tow."

They started speed-walking.

Clarissa tugged at the purple Dunn-Blatt tie dangling from Sarah's wrist. Clarissa said, "Was it not weird? Primaries should have appeared to bear witness to the Shenanigan Challenge?"

Sullen, Sarah shook her head. "You weren't hooked, Clarissa." A shiver ran through her. "You don't know what they were planning to do."

"What?" The blonde's hair touched her shoulder when she tilted her head with the question.

Sarah looked down to the tie. "I should have demanded his keys and hood."

Walking between rows of cars, Ben shifted his eyes from the girls to the dark wagon in the distance. The faint candle light within made the moving shadows on the curtains dance in odd ways. Tying back into the conversation, he said, "Those guys are perfect examples of why Dunn-Blatt's practitioners have the bad reputation." He looked to Clarissa. "They were out to do harm."

His peripheral vision registered Sarah nodding to support his statement.

An air of innocence and naiveté clung to Clarissa, and if her friend wasn't going to explain to her that the Primaries didn't show because the boys were issuing challenges far more sinister then the Samhain Shenanigan, Ben decided he wasn't going to either.

Clarissa didn't grasp the situation and her brown eyes begged for a solid answer.

Trying to clue her in, Ben changed his mind. *Maybe*

she'll get it if I lay a sugar-coated trail for her to follow. "They probably, *probably*, would have stolen your tablets."

"That's just silly." Clarissa's eyes rolled as she quickly rambled, "Why would they steal our schoolwork? Our school's enchantment focus is nearly the opposite of theirs. Heck, we don't even have comparable classes. Further, why would they think I would bring it to the Samhain Celebration? That's just —" Her face tightened up as though the word forming in her mouth tasted sour. She blinked hard as though she had to fight to get the word out. "—stupid."

Sarah tapped Clarissa's arm and spoke in a gentle manner. "He means our bracers, dear."

Clarissa faced changed to shocked fear. She pulled her right arm into her chest and covered it tightly with her left. "Why would they do that?"

Sarah didn't respond.

"So you won't have them." Ben said, as he took a last look at the wagon. It became obscured by other wagons and trailers. "Well, that and to reap what they can from the spell memory."

Clarissa dropped her arms. "Huh?"

"He means, echo-cast." Sarah translated as her eyes went to Ben's Anvilsmith for a moment before returning to the tie. "We don't cast the way Apes do."

Apes? Even after I helped them out of a bind. The last thing he expected to hear from them was the horrible slur. Ben stopped. *Don't be rude in return.* He told himself again. *Ben, don't be rude in return.* He fought hard to squash the urge. Trying to squeeze the sudden anger away, he jammed his hands in his coat pocket and made tight fists.

Sarah glanced back, stopped, and turned. Realizing what she had said, her eyes widened and she sucked her bottom lip between her teeth, making her apology come out slushy. "Shit, shorry."

"Perhaps you girls should go on without me." Ben shrugged. *Keep cool.* He tried to seem aloof while his fists were clenching and unclenching. He wanted to prove the superiority of his style of casting, but flaunting skill stood against the Archon Private Academy's Charter, which he never understood since dueling—the ultimate form of casters showing off their skill—had brought techno-casting from zero to its current stature.

When the method was being pioneered in 1984, the entire Tradition mocked using technology to cast spells. At first, it had been slow and the spells were weak. *Traditional casters* collectively declared, "It was so easy, that a monkey could do it." Which gave rise to anti-tech posters of monkeys at computers, and *the slur*.

In 1992, *The Shroud*, a caster wrapped mummy-like, with thick hooded robes, took to The Circuit with a mundane laptop modified by Gnomecraft Artificers— later upgraded to tablets—and held The Circuit Crown until 2002. When The Shroud finally removed his coverings and revealed himself as Master Reynolds. The starwise world was infuriated. He had been the first in centuries to break vows to the Queen-Mother's Monastery. Cast out as a pariah, he had risen to be a champion and opened his own school, the first Archon Primary Academy.

Ben's hands stopped working. "Maybe one day, we *Apes* will be allowed to participate in the Junior Circuit. Then we'll see what we'll see."

As she had in the parking lot, Sarah took a step toward him. This time, she extended her hands, palms up, a foot from her hips. She wanted to take his hand to lower her forehead to it in apology.

Recognizing the courtly gesture, Ben stepped back to deny her. Logically, he felt like he had dismissed the anger the slur brought, but the Nilosian energy in his head burned the word in his brain as though she had branded him. Bastion wouldn't let him get over it. Ben pointed. "The opening to the fairgrounds is right up there."

She pouted and made a second attempt.

A sneer turned Ben's lips as he shifted further away. *If you think you're looks could make me forgive the egregious insult, you've got another thing coming.* He shook his head. "No, we're done." As an afterthought, he cursed Bastion.

Because of the beast reinforcing the insult, Ben knew he was being a complete ass, but couldn't stop.

He'd been so focused on keeping Sarah at bay that he didn't notice Clarissa bound forward until she slid her arms around his sides. Inside his coat, she had him wrapped in a hug, and planted a quick kiss on his cheek before going back to hugging him. She spoke into his chest. "Thank you, Benjamin Baxter."

Furious at Sarah, Ben was about to shove Clarissa away when the purity of her gratitude shook Bastion's manipulation and shrank Ben's anger to a manageable proportion. Ben closed his arms around her and returned the embrace. "You're welcome, Clarissa."

Sarah started to move forward to turn the moment into group affection.

No. He extended his hand, palm out.

Sarah stopped. Her eyes turned a careless roll. "Come on, Clarissa."

The blonde dragged her arms against Ben's sides as she released him to catch up with her friend.

Before they'd gotten too far from him, Ben remembered Jack's treachery. He verified the Anvilsmith still hung from his hip and ran a finger across his spellcard holder. Nothing had been taken.

The girls entered the fairground.

Ben turned back to the parking lot to look over the few remaining cars of the starwise who had to park in the mundane lot. Near three A.M., the mundane part of the carnival had closed. Though he could not see from the outside, a large number of duels—the festival's main draw—were taking place just on the other side of the entrance. These two weeks of light-hearted contests were the only ones in which the Archon Private Academy could partake; the normal stigmas forgotten in the spirit of Samhain.

The gruff voice came from his ring again. "Return to Meadows Towing."

"I will. I will." Ben removed the ring and put it in a pocket. He didn't know what the orcs needed, but his parents only allowed him to come to the festival this one night. If he'd stuck to his plan of only playing a few round of the Conjuror's Course and gone home with tickets, his dad probably would've talked his mom into letting him come back... Now, empty handed, he'd have to sneak to come back; which he loathed to do.

Ben stopped playing the *if* game. He had one night —tonight—to have fun and he'd yet to see Crystal's idol, Papa Mojo, for the free reading she had arranged. To soothe his mind for not immediately responding to the ring summons, Ben spoke to himself. "If it's of dire importance, they'll call."

Walking to the entrance, Ben raised his right arm to show he did not have a Shenanigans armband and moved onto the fairgrounds.

Though the APA sanctioned these bouts, his parents consistently refused to sign the disclosure, waiver, and consent forms... Which sucked. Ben tried to find the bright side of not participating in the games. "At least there won't be a line for the Seer." Failing at minimizing his desire to duel, he added, "If he's still open."

A hook landed just below his ribs and traveled to his sternum. His hand shot to his spellcards before he felt the jovial spirit of the person who had hooked him. Turning sideways, he looked down the taught emerald tether to see Clarissa. Color filled her dimpled cheeks and her small smile spread ever so slightly wider when her intent to duel him for a kiss registered.

His own cheeks beginning to warm, Ben smiled back.

Whirling gray robes appeared next to her. The Vibrosian Primary appeared. The Magistrate's gaze traveled down the tether to him with his hand held high in unquestionable non-participation. She pointed her baton at Clarissa.

Clarissa tried to unhook him.

Ben wanted to hold on to flirt with her, but he'd already been given a censure warning. Another strike might get him booted from the festival for the night.

He let his intent of wanting to hold on be known through the tether and let the hook go.

The Magistrate waved at Ben to move on to the safe zone in the starwise section of the fair.

He started walking.

Though he couldn't hear what she was saying, the Vibrosian Primary took to scolding Clarissa. Something about the excessive finger waggling made the Magistrate look like she moved beyond acting in official capacity. He'd never heard of this kind of thing happening. Was a Sunrise Mountain girl liking a technocaster that offensive? Ben couldn't help wondering aloud, "What's up with that?"

Chapter Twelve

UNDER SURVEILLANCE

BEN'S PLAN of returning to the dark wagon vanished when he viewed the anemic crowds inside the starwise area. Being generous with his guess, Ben figured only a tenth of the former crowd had been non-teens and these adults, and children, were the only ones still wondering around. Seemingly, without exception, everyone able to participate in the Shenanigans—the uncountable mass of teens—were. The thinned out crowd meant fewer games in operation, which, in turn, meant the released workers would be in the employee only area.

The Adults milling around, most with children too young to participate in the duels, eyed him—*the last teen on Earth, a pimple on an otherwise flawless face* —suspiciously.

"Ben," Gary called out. *Challenge the Conjurer* proved to be one of the few games that still had a decent line. He held up the bags of Ben's SD cards.

Even against the odds, a part of Ben wanted to try to make it back to where Collins and the woman talked about him. If he took the bags, they would slow him down or give him away if he had to leave them behind. Ben shook his head. "Can you hold onto them?"

"Sure." Gary set the bags down and began to make his way back up to his booth. "Have fun and keep an eye out for the dragon's assault."

"Will do," Ben replied as his mind started working on what the parting term could have meant. *Dragon's assault. Doubtlessly code for something…* Ben snapped his fingers. *Got it!*

Though he never went for it, Ben had asked Gary about the top spell at the *Conjuror's Course*. Wearing the attendant uniform instead of his current harlequin worker's robs, Gary had poo-pooed the prize, stating a dragon conjuration was no good if the caster didn't also know dragon tactics. Most didn't know how to fight dragon-style and always tried to start their attack from behind their target and over cover.

When Ben turned to scan the building and tent tops behind him, a bright orange scrying sensor dropped below the edge.

So far, he'd only seen the one Vibrosian Primary. *Is she keeping tabs on me?* He had to make sure he wasn't just being paranoid. Ben made his way through the midway and into the Fae Fort Food Court. *Holy…* Most of the booths were closed, but Southern Sweets had a sign out front. *We want to be in on the Shenanigans, too. If you want to play, but can't, come get a free Cotton Cloud.* Then in smaller print. *Offer only valid for school-aged practitioners.*

Feeling a bit foolish standing in lines with pre-teens, Ben waited his turn and ordered his favorite, a

Kamikaze. The pie-faced lady smiled widely at him and spun him the largest serving of cotton candy Ben had seen. Before accepting, he bowed deeply and thank her. Made with all thirty available base flavors, his confection had a random pattern like a crazy, tie-dyed t-shirt with colors that ranged from white to deep brown. Strolling between the midway and Fae Fort Food Court, and back again, he tilted his head to eat the delicious sugar cloud. By the time he finished the massive thing, he had secretly spied the sensor a dozen times more. *Why is the Primary keeping tabs on me?*

Under direct surveillance, Ben had no chance of returning to the dark wagon without giving her a reason to fixate on him further.

He had only been an Initiate at the time, but he clearly remembered the three, bright red scry sensors that followed a near-graduating APA student everywhere. Later, when he had asked Adept Matton why, the Adept said the student was Geotheon Mossburge—as though the name alone would be answer enough. It had been Ben's first time seeing sensors and, as such, he figured they always came in threes. Time proved otherwise. Three Magistrates kept tabs on Geotheon at all times. *What had Geotheon done?*

Heck, what did I do?

Even if he managed to fish his ring from his pocket on the sly, he'd probably suddenly vanish from her extrasensory field of vision.

Though not illegal, hiding from a Primary's scry would be akin to waving an *I'm up to no good* flag, as the mystical sensors were the Magistrates' main form of patrolling the city. He had heard that you were presumed innocent until they could prove you guilty, but if you tried to evade the Lesser Judges, the presumption switched.

Having seen how they responded to Collins' spell, he knew the latter half to be true.

Ben gave up on spying on the Senior Adept, and hoped Papa Mojo's had stayed open. *Perhaps the seer can tell me why the Primary has taken such an interest in me.*

Chapter Thirteen

PAPA MOJO

DIM LIGHTS LIT THE LONG, French Quarter-esqe, Diviner's Row. Various wagons of different designs were all packed tightly together to make the most of their limited section of the Samhain Festival. This late, all of the wagons were closed and the merchandise had been cleared away from most of the stands.

Figuring he wasn't far from the truth, Ben identified the ones he thought were the best at divination by their racks still having wares on display. Those rare few wagons might as well have had a sign posted that said *go ahead and steal, you'll be caught!* Some even had Everbloom flowering plants out front, battling for scent superiority. Roses versus sunflowers versus honey suckle. Nature's battle royal.

Ben stopped before the wagon he found to be the most colorful.

Its bright yellow base had grass and long green stems painted up the side, blossoming into clouds. The white-trim gutter of the roof above the front door rained hundreds of tiny bubbles. Four pinwheels set to the four directions squeaked softly as they all rotated clockwise. Instead of a trinket stand, there were rows and rows of wrapped candy with a real sign, reading *Have one.*

He smiled, picked a small, root beer barrel hard candy, and made a mental note to return here next year. With the chaotic taste of the delicious Kamikaze cotton candy still swimming in his mouth, he tucked the barrel away and hustled past the remaining wagons to the very end, where Crystal said Papa Mojo's cart would be.

Its glow more obvious in the darkened row, the Primary's orange sensor stayed behind the wagons, but kept pace.

To Ben's mild surprise, the row ended in a chain-link fence. He had expected a wagon.

Ben compared the two wagons which were pressed up against the fence, bowing it slightly. Both were dirty, had their lights out, and were made of dark, weathered wood. Neither had trinket stands or any other form of attention-getters out front. The only difference between them lay in the layer of dirt packed in every imperfection on the left-hand wagon. Both were aged, but the left one suffered from willful neglect.

As he turned toward it, a rope dropped before the chain-link fence. A deep, gravelly voice with a New Orleans drawl drifted down. "Benjamin. Crystal has told me about you."

Ben studied the rope. The bottom hung just above the ground and the top appeared to be suspended in midair. Grabbing hold, he gave it a shake. The bottom flopped freely, but the top point remained anchored to something he couldn't quite perceive. The hair on the back of his neck began to rise. Ben asked, "Do I climb up?"

"Depends," the voice answered, then asked, "Do you want a reading?"

What has Crystal signed me up for? Putting one hand above the other, Ben pulled on the rope to jump and heave his body up, and was about to wrap his legs around it when the area changed.

He still held the rope, but the top had loosened from its anchor point, and went limp in his hands.

Ben stood inside a darkened room. The lack of lighting made the area into an optical illusion as though he stood in infinite darkness. He put his hand in front of his face and couldn't see it. A part of him felt that if he were to extend his arms, he would probably be able to touch both walls. About to do so, an odor—a cross of mildew and acrid mothballs—crept into his nose.

Once idle in the font of Nilosian energy concentrated in Ben's head, Bastion roused.

The beast's apprehension translated through Ben as he lowered into a defensive stance. His hand went to the spellcard holder placing his index finger on Shield, his middle on Blast, and his thumb on Orion. Turning a slow circle, a faintly glowing sphere suspended in air at the far end of the room, caught his attention.

Something dark and slim settled on the other side of the sphere. The lighting from the orb barely lit a two-inch radius around it. A face, only visible from just under the nose, leaned forward, throwing shadows across the cheeks and higher. The pools of shadows in the eye sockets parted to a deeper darkness. Eyes opened, the face appeared to be a porcelain mask suspended just behind the orb of light.

The mouth moved and the same deep slow voice from the top of the rope rolled to him. "Come forward, Benjamin. I won't bite."

Instead of doing as beckoned, Ben paid attention to Bastion. The beast—Ben started to think of as his Nilosian personification—seemed leery, but had not become fully active.

Ben kept his fingers on his spellcards, sliding his pinky to Feather's Grace in case he fell into a pit or a trap door opened beneath him as he inched through the dark room. The floor gave slight resistance as though he walked on deep, plush carpet. He looked down again, but the darkness obscured everything not lit by the orb.

As he moved closer to the light source, the shape of the crystal ball on a squat black base registered. It lit the center of a checkered purple and black wooden table with chess pieces around it. The mildewed mothball smell grew stronger.

Ben couldn't recall the crystal ball that Crystal used ever glowing, but, then again, she never had all of the lights out in her apartment.

Proximity revealed precious little more of the face. The mouth—*not a mask, then. Ivory skin?*—moved with the words. "I am Papa Mojo. My visions are faultless. What I see cannot be questioned and cannot be denied." As though feeling Ben scrutinizing him, the face withdrew into the shadows to fade from view. "For what I see will always come to be."

Shielding his mind as Elder Komir taught him, Ben

imagined his thoughts and memories secured in a thick iron box. He did this mostly for protection, but his inner skeptic began searching for faults. *Can I trust someone who obscures themselves in shadows?*

"Sit across the table from me." Papa Mojo bayed and the shape of a folding chair moved in the darkness. "Let my crystal ball see you so that we may divine what your future holds."

Ready to react to an attack or sinister laugh, Ben sat on the shadow chair.

Chapter Fourteen

FUTURE TELLING

BEN HAD SEEN a classic horror movie which ended when a teenage caster sought out a mad witch to divine the outcome of—what he thought would be his worst decision—leaving the starwise world to join the mundane. When the caster looked into the witch's crystal ball, he saw himself looking in on himself, looking in on himself, and when he looked up, he only saw the witch's face—monstrously huge, concaved, and laughing—looking down at him trapped inside her orb. The credits rolled.

Though the darkness in Papa Mojo's dank wagon kept the exact dimensions from being known, something about the darkness seemed to press in tight around the glowing crystal ball. The weight of shadows triggered a concern in Ben that could easily blossom into a full claustrophobic fear.

The mask—*white face paint slathered thick on his forehead, cheekbones, and chin*—drew a bit closer to the orb where Ben could make out the darker areas of the eyes. Doing his best to make light of the steadily increasing thump of his heart flooding his system with adrenaline, Ben spoke in the same airy cadence as Papa Mojo. "What do you see, for me?"

Dark irises, recessed further back in the painted face than Ben had thought, flicked from the orb, to him, and then returned to fixate on the crystal ball.

Ready to defend himself—*if you try to capture my soul...*—Ben pressed his lips together and swallowed.

The face floated back and away from the crystal ball as long, skeletal fingers—*four joints? Five?*—closed in on the light which never lit Papa Mojo's palms.

Almost subconsciously, Ben nodded a confessional agreement to his imagination that the worst nightmare it could conjure for him tonight would involve those impossibly long, disembodied fingers threatening to close tight around his neck when he closed his eyes to sleep.

Papa Mojo's voice rumbled across the table, "She likes you, but you and Crystal are not destined."

What the heck is he talking about? Ben felt his features tightened. *Not destined for what?*

Papa Mojo's floating face eased toward the light a little. The darkness made his white face paint look like something created from dingy gray papier-mâché. "Nor are you to be with Sarah."

My love life? Really? Ben's mouth curled into a smirk. Relationships were the first place unskilled diviners went to try and wow the customer with their ability to say—*not an ability to see the future*—what the customer wanted to hear. Nothing less than the world would have to be at stake for him to date the Sunrise Mountain elitist. Anything less could burn. Ben sighed. *How could Crystal see so much in this guy? He starts with a near slam dunk topic while not getting close to anything that I really want to know?*

Leaning in to interrupt and ask about the Vibrosian's sensor, Ben's tongue froze to the roof of his mouth when the mystic's fingers stopped moving and pulled away from the light. "Nor Clarissa."

Closer, floating inside Papa Mojo's scrying device, a fluid scene of the hug Clarissa had sprung on him replayed from a floating point of view which showed Sarah off to the side. Clarissa's eyes were closed as she pressed the side of her face again his chest. They remained closed as she lifted her face to peck-kiss his check before returning to the hug. From this angle, Ben could see her slip something into his pocket as they separated.

He slipped his hand into his coat and felt a small rectangle of stiff paper. Suddenly, a subtle fear of looking up and seeing Papa Mojo's masked face monstrously huge, concaved, and laughing—*just like in the movie*—settled on his shoulders like a freezing yoke.

The image wafted away as Mojo's fingers returned to working the orb.

Ben stole a glance up at the mask and, upon seeing the white paint turned dingy in the dark, breathed a bit easier.

Miniscule glints lit in Mojo's eyes as the orb brightened. "This is who you want to be with."

Cursing himself while he did so—*I might fall in*—Ben leaned in closer to the orb. A fond smile filled his face as a Penelope montage played inside the magical orb—Tex cutting open the burlap bag she had been stuffed in and removing her thumbscrews. Penelope standing in the back of his car while casting the spell which made the Transcend fly. Penelope walking through Pepperjacks. Penelope being chased by the dragon-tuzvul. Penelope covering her mouth at what she saw in the huge war scene painting. The meal they shared with Elder Komir. Penelope hiding in the stable and watching him fight Jack, and then—flash— Penelope in her gold and crimson robes at a desk looking into a crystal ball of her own.

"This didn't happen," Ben said. At least he didn't think it had. Trying to see what she was doing with her own crystal ball, Ben leaned over the table, even closer to Papa Mojo's orb. "What's she doing there?"

Mojo's fingers worked around the orb, at times millimeters in front of Ben's face, tracing symbols in the air. "I cannot tell." His deep voice sounded strained. "The wards in the room she's in are too strong."

Penelope turned in her chair to look up at them.

Instead of washing away like the others visions, this image flickered out to black. Then the crystal ball slowly lit again.

Ben's flushed with heat. He sat bolt upright and gripped the edge of the table. "Will I see her again?"

Papa Mojo's face faded back into darkness as the hands closed in on the sphere. Those long fingers nearly encircled the crystal ball, the diviner's palms were coated in the same white paint and came a hair's breadth from making contact. A hiss filled the area as Mojo's hands shook. Swirling red and black smoke whirled inside the orb. It rolled, undulated, and switched directions. Mojo's painted face shot toward the crystal ball. He blew on the glass.

Thick and voluminous, Ben could smell the contents. Smoldering *ashes*. It brought back the month-old memory of Pepperjacks burning. Then, that tangy sweet smell of freshly sawed and varnished wood.

The ball cleared.

Ben saw himself—the same—and Penelope—dark, curly hair flowing down from a golden, ruby encrusted, circlet set high on her head. They stood, together, outside Pepperjacks' front doors, newly remade front crimson stained glass. *The future.* She stepped forward. Ben licked his lips for a kiss. She reached out and shook his hand.

A quick surge of air puffed from Ben's lips. His dreamy hope of seeing her again, a reoccurring fantasy, burst. He sighed. "A flippin' handshake? That's all?"

Papa Mojo's fingers worked in quick motions and pulled back into darkness. The handshake grew to fill the crystal ball.

Ben's shoulders slumped at the sight of her red leather-clad hand in his. "She's even wearing gloves."

Papa Mojo's deep voice rumbled, "She knows what you are and the type of magic you were born to use."

What'd he just say? Ben's guts turned to ice. They churned in fear. Shook in anger. *Shouldn't have let my guard down.* Using black magic would make one an outcast, but being a true Nilosian—which he had discovered he was and could not undo, *so unfair*—would get you killed, and he'd been discovered.

A quick mental inventory found his protection still in place. *I didn't let my guard down. Wait, he said 'she* knows.' *Mojo may not.* Ready to fight for his life, Ben lifted his gaze from the crystal ball to the diviner.

Still white-faced, thin snake-like slits slashed through dull yellow orbs set in the dark hollows of Papa Mojo's eye sockets. Mojo rumbled, "It is my magic, too, Benjamin." His thin digits went to the light from the crystal ball. Black magic oozed from the fingertips like ink squirted into water before being sucked back in. "I show you now, for you will find out before you see me again. We are now joined in darkness, Brother." Papa Mojo bridged his fingers over the crystal ball, forefingers stippled between the reptilian eyes. "I cannot expose *you*, for you would reveal *me*."

Ben breathed a little easier for a moment. He tensed. *I'm in an accord with him.*

Leaning back, a dark cavernous maw, highlighted by the white face paint on the dark diviner's chin, grew when the man smiled. "Even the handshake may not happen if you do not last through tonight and save Clarissa tomorrow."

"What's happening tonight?" Ben's mind shifted from concern about his safety to worry for Clarissa's survival. *She's probably the only truly innocent person I know.* "What's happening tomorrow?"

"Purple on a car..." Papa Mojo's fingers dropped back to working the crystal ball. Malcolm, in a deep violet, hardtop Transcend—*he has the same car as me*—with a charging buffalo painted along the length. Mojo hummed before waving his hands. Malcolm, and his car, flew away in wafts of smoke. "Not that one." Another vehicle appeared, a trembling white

Legerity muscle car with a dark magenta trunk and bumper.

Ben scanned the car vibrating from the stock, oversized engine crammed in and cranked up. *There's no identifiers on the car. Beyond the paint there, there was nothing to make it look different than any other Legerity.*

Mojo rolled his fingers around the ball. Inside, a flash of Ben, in his black Transcend, following the Legerity. "Chase this car." A flash of red taillights disappearing around an impossibly tight corner. "It will lose you in an industrial complex where Clarissa is being packed and shipped." Another flash. Ben smiled at seeing himself laying a body wrapped in burlap —*why do they use burlap*—in his backseat. His small robotic companion, Tex, was there and had to move quickly to get out of the way.

Papa Mojo waved at the vision. The Legerity came back for a moment before it puffed away into slow-moving white and purple smoke. His eyes dimmed to a darkened burnt yellow. "You won't have time to free her then. Whether you see them or not, her abductors will pursue until you get back here. Get her to the starwise entrance and she'll be safe."

Ben arced an eyebrow. "How will that make her safe?"

"We will be one day closer to Samhain." Papa Mojo answered, "There will be even more Magistrates on duty and one will see you race onto the fairgrounds. Then, after that one shows, they will all come."

"Okay." Ben nodded. He'd seen the Primaries at work a couple of times and they did run in packs. "So, what about tonight?"

As though he no longer needed the divining device, Papa Mojo moved his hands away from the crystal ball. The slightest remaining hint of his yellow eyes faded and shadows filled the seer's sockets. "The orcs are in trouble, but you'll have to weigh helping them versus exposing Collins for what he truly is."

Senior Adept Collins? Ben sat up straight. His mouth wetted. He swallowed. "What is he?"

"Expose him…" The face and fingers withdrew from the light. Papa Mojo drew a shallow breath and let it out with a wheeze. "…and find out. This session," The seer drew in a much deeper breath and exhaled, "is over."

The crystal ball went dark, so did the room.

A door creaked behind Ben. Bright illumination spilled in throwing his shadow across the table, blotting out the crystal ball, Papa Mojo, and his long creepy fingers. A cheery voice, as sweet as jelly beans, called over the brilliant P. A. system. "Attention, Benjamin Baxter."

Ben glanced over his shoulder.

With an otherworldly *pop*—which rang on Ben's ears —the darkness of Mojo's wagon burst like a balloon.

He stood right where the rope had dropped down in front of him between the weathered wagons at the end of Diviner's Row. The announcer continued, "Please report to Red Lot Five. Your tow is here."

Ben had many more questions before Mojo went *completely spent* on him.

Why do seer end sessions like that? This wasn't the first time a diviner had called a session done on Ben before he was ready. *Wonder if it's an act to keep the customer from asking for too much, or if spending arcane energy to glimpse the future is truly that taxing.*

The perky voice repeated the call for him to respond for his tow. Doing as directed, Ben began to make his way over to starwise parking. *But I'm not parked in Red Lot Five, and I don't need a tow...*

THRILLED to have fresh festival air—*I still want popcorn*—
instead of the heavy, manure smell of his shortcut
through the Mystic Menagerie, Ben took in a deep
breath. *The animals may be magical, but their poop still
stinks.* Ben took another deep breath to clear his lungs.
His gazed settled across the long paved spans. He could
see each of the five entrances from the Red, White, and
Black starwise lots.

Before midnight, this area would be full of Samhain
entertainers aiming to excite incoming festival goers
and a person would be lucky to see fifty feet ahead of
themselves. This late, the bare area almost felt sad. For
the first time, Ben noticed the shape of large wild cats—
there's a whole lot of lions—in the lengths of beautifully
crafted, wrought iron fences separating the entrances.
Beyond the fences, several Koffman Lanterns floated
out in the dark parking lot, floating twenty-five feet
above casters leaving the festival and illuminating the
area around them.

Furthest away, under two ornate lion paws supporting a large glowing red "Five," Ben could make out the Vibrosian Primary, Collins, and Jek waiting for him. The Magistrate stood so straight, Ben would've guessed her baton was up her butt if she didn't have it pointed at him. Next to her, Collins. The Senior Adept tried to emulate the Primary's commanding presence, but failed to rise higher than simply being demanding. Quite a bit taller than both casters, Jek stood hunched in the white Meadows Towing t-shirt and blue jeans. The bearded orc had his neck bent and his thick, orcish brow cast foreboding shadows over his eyes.

A series of yells, students raising their voices to call out their school's name, in attempts to drown out all the other pulsed from further in the grounds. About to yell out himself, Ben stopped. No one was around that would appreciate him calling out *A. P. A.*, nor compete against him by voicing their own school. Not inside or taking part in creating the din, their rhythmic voices sounded like a cacophony of the insane.

Ben paused. It occurred to him that Jek was the only orc—*heck, the only non-human*—he had ever seen at the Samhain Festival. Broadening his scope, the reality of the entire city not having one non-human, besides Collin's elf, smacked him.

How could that be, when there was a towing company with only orcs as employees, and a giant inside of Pepperjacks?

Ben pulled his Anvilsmith and made a note to ask Councilor Eastly about this phenomenon at their monthly review. Sliding his tablet back on his hip, Ben felt no pressure to rush to the casters, but he had a feeling time was of the essence for his orcs.

Tone lofty and demanding, the Primary spoke first. She said, "Have you seen either of the Sunrise Mountain girls you followed into the fairgrounds recently?"

"You should know," Ben snapped. "You've been watching me since."

Her eyebrows lowered to draw a *you're-testing-my-patience* line between them.

Unabashed, Ben held her gaze.

Her lips pursed into a tight seal. They split to let out a single, strained, word. "Tone."

Ben tightened his throat to bar his sarcastic replies. He'd rushed headlong into a social faux pas. Years of following the rules, pressing his heels together in acknowledgment. *What would happen if I refused to bow?* Only a fleeting thought. Ben bowed at the waist until he bent at thirty degrees. He noted dust and dirt clinging to the hem of her outermost gray robe. *What have you been up to, Magistrate?* Softening his voice to a respectful tone, Ben said, "My apologies, Lesser Judge."

Her voice remained stressed. "A representative from your school is here, and I am certain he will make sure your *Courtmanship* Adept is made aware of this folly."

She didn't acknowledge my apology. Ben held his position. Though she had stopped speaking, he was to hold the position until she gave him permission to stand. She was testing his adherence to tradition and, probably because of his small act of defiance, waited in silence to impress her status upon him.

Inwardly, Ben frowned. *She's not worthy of the office.*

Oh, crap. He focused to steel his thoughts, which were protected behind thick layers. Thankfully, he had shielded them out of habit.

Bastion stirred from his slumber in Ben's head and began a round of rebellious hoots.

Unfamiliar with the social rigors of magic-using society, and not knowing to be still until the highest ranking person gave permission to move, Jek shifted from foot to foot. A sound like two pieces of sandpaper rubbing together came from the orc.

Ben didn't shift his eyes—that would put him in deeper water—but from his peripheral vision, he could see the orc wringing his thick hands.

The Magistrate must have given Collins a nod, as the Senior Adept's brown cowboy boots sauntered into view. "Care to make another attempt, *Junior* Adept?" Collins' normally condescending tone felt heavier, but oddly not as personal.

Attempt at what? Apologizing? Ben blinked, making sure he didn't keep his eyes closed for too long or the power-tripping jerks would rightfully suspect him of entertaining unpleasant thoughts about them.

Bastion bounded around his head urging Ben to act on those thoughts. With Jek present, they could easy beat down the two mages and scram.

And go where? They'll hunt us. Ben said, "I decline."

"Noted." Collins' boots moved away before he prompted, "Then answer the Lesser Judge."

"I have not—" Ben managed to keep his voice even and his tone respectful. Further he kept his jaw loose to not show how much having to say these honorific words pissed him off. "My Lady."

She waved the baton under his nose, granting him permission to stand straight, and whirled her robes. In a suck of air, nature filling a vacuum, she teleported away.

"That was bullshit." Ben had not meant for the words to come out, but they did as he straightened and gained eye contact with Collins.

Free to return to his bitter demeanor, the Senior Adept said, "What did you say *Junior*—"

"What she did." Fuming, Ben extended a hand to where the Primary had been, and cut in. "I didn't do anything wrong." Wanting to leave, he took a step toward Jek. "Complete and utter bullshit, and didn't serve a purpose."

Collins hissed, "It was much-needed, to remind you of your place." His boot scrapped on the pavement. "Hey, Baxter, I didn't dismiss—"

Jek shuffled.

Collins *oofed* a surprised puff of air.

He turned to see the Senior Adept several feet away, sitting on the ground. Still, next to Ben, Jek brought his arms back from full extension. Ben's neck swiveled as he locked between the two, piecing together the scenario. Collins must have advanced on him to grab his arm like they were at the Archon Private Academy, but Jek had interceded, shoving the Senior Adept to the ground.

Staring death at Jek, Collins jumped back to his feet. Hot and dangerous, his voice came from deep in his throat. "How dare you, cur?" Abnormal bumps moved behind the flesh around Collins' mouth as though he had grown fangs. They showed when Collins thundered, "You will learn your place!"

Having seen Collins blast students not allowed to defend against the attack at school, Ben slipped his hand to the SD card on his hip. He stepped in front of Jek and channeled Argosian into it. "He's no student of yours."

Instead of a mystic bolt blasting from the Senior Adept's hand, neutered fizzing crimson smoke puffed from his fingertips and faded. Collins' jaw clenched tight. The pupil in his right eye cracked. Inky black flooded the blue iris.

The Senior Adept's face changed in an instant. His absolute rage became abject horror as his hand slapped over his eye socket.

Though quick, Ben didn't doubt what he saw.

"Loyalty, from an orc..." Muttering the rest, Collins turned away to flee.

"Don't use that word, Collins." Ben called as the Senior Adept's boots carried him away. Having waited for an opportunity to address Collins slipping him a cursed tablet, Ben chided, "I'm sure it burns your mouth."

Collins stopped. Lips still moving as he talked to himself, the Senior Adept looked back at Ben with his inky eye covered. Boots clicking, Collins continued to hurry away.

Ben wanted to chase Collins down. To flag anyone they came across to expose the Senior Adept's inky eye, doubtlessly full of Nilosian energy.

Papa Mojo's prediction came back to him. *The orcs*

are in trouble, but you'll have to weigh helping them versus exposing Collins for what he truly is.

Knowing he had to choose between the two didn't make the decision any easier, but it did enable Ben to make his choice quicker. He pulled his tablet, typed a command to Tex, and motioned for Jek to take the lead. "Where's your truck?"

Chapter Sixteen
A TOUGH CONCEPT

WINDOW ROLLED DOWN, Ben had his arm hanging on the passenger side window of Jek's tow truck. The cool night air whipped his sleeve back, and every time they hit a bump too hard, he reeled his arm in to check the side mirror and made sure his Transcend was still hooked on the back.

Ben didn't share the orcs confidence in the tow chains. Even with both windows down, the cab still held the slight, persistent smell of freshly-sliced salami. Getting a tenuous grip on the situation, Ben peered into the darkness just beyond Jek's high beams.

Driving in silence, the orc kept both of his hands on the rocking, sheepskin-covered steering wheel. Waiting for the next question, he occasionally glanced at Ben.

For his part, Ben understood the basic tenants of orcs being either slaves or wild. Jek had done his best to give the short version of the reason why all the goblinoid races—weebos, goblins, orcs, hobgoblins, ubbos—all embraced *slave or wild* as a way of life. It had been the main reason his orcs decided to stay and *serve* rather than accepting their freedom when Ben had offered it to them.

Jek made a quick right turn.

After making sure his car hadn't broken free, Ben caught a visual of the Meadows Towing rotating, bright neon purple, star sign. He gave up wrestling with the concept to cut to summation. "So, this guy wants to challenge me for the scrapyard."

"No, Ben." Jek uttered a soft groan. "Just the title."

Almost feeling like a part of the *Who's on First* comic routine, Ben confirmed, "Might-Fist?"

"Yes." Jek nodded. "Exactly." The orc's nod looked tired, as though Jek had grown weary from trying to repeatedly explain something so simple.

Ben said, "All right." Pressing a finger on the sheepskin-covered dashboard with each fact, Ben gave understanding another shot. "Okay, the title gains him the belt. The belt gives him dominion over Meadows Towing." Jek opened his mouth to interject, but Ben rushed on. "Which makes *him* the Might-Fist. Once he's Might-Fist, he can turn ownership of the scrapyard to whomever he chooses by giving them the belt, but he'd still retain the title."

Jek gave a strong nod. "By Krilliloas, you got it!"

Ben tried to think of a way this could be handled peacefully. Nothing tangible came. *If an accord is struck, and I relent, there's no way to assure the deal would be upheld.* Defensive of how long it took him to get it, Ben explained, "I was likening it to human battle-sports, where the title and belt are inseparable."

Jek cut his eyes away. "This isn't a sport, Ben."

"Oh, trust me, I know." *Boy do I know.* Ben looked at the remaining eighty-five arcane watts on his tablet. "So, if I take this guy out—"

"When!" Jek corrected and slapped the steering wheel as though he squashed a bug. "*When* you do, his warriors stop fighting." The orc clenched his fist in victory. "And all of his possessions become yours."

Ben looked to the rotating purple star. "So, those are the rules."

"More like magical traditions." Jek stressed, "But only for the title."

Feeling a bit slow, Ben said, "Got it."

Within range, the orc pressed the gate opener strapped with rubber bands to his tattered sun visor. "You'd have to dominate his men into service." A casual single-shoulder shrug lulled Jek's head to the side. "Kill a few of the more defiant ones. That'll bring the rest quickly under heel."

As they drove onto the property, Ben's heart dropped. His neck tightened and his voice became small. "Thing is, I don't want to kill anyone."

In contrast, since hearing of the challenge, Bastion had swirled into a mass of pent-up rage in Ben's head, begging to be released.

Ben cleared his throat to loosen his tightening vocal chords. "So, they can't just murder me on sight, right?"

Another passive shrug. Jek's lack of concern started to become worrisome. Jek said, "He could, but then the title wouldn't transfer."

Afraid to ask, Ben did, "What would happen then?"

Jek answered, "Then, whoever defeats him, and

pries it from his hands *and* defends the belt ten times, becomes the rightful Might-Fist of the area."

Hearing how bloody the process could be, Ben tried —for a moment—to imagine how many creatures had died on this ground for either the stupid belt or lofty title. In his mind's eye, the thought turned the numerous columns of countless wrecked cars into mounds of dead bodies. A shudder ran through him. "Why'd he even come?" Ben's budding paranoia —*thanks Collins*—searched for a reason. "I mean, why tonight?"

Jek dug in his left ear. "Last he heard, his father was the Might-Fist." The orc looked at the ear wax in his pinky nail for a moment before rubbing it into his seat. "As all good vassals will do, he came to pay tribute and discovered that his dad is dead—"

"Imprisoned," Ben cut in. "Not dead." He parted some of the sheepskin on the dashboard to indicate the subtle difference and defend himself. As much as he could, he had been humane to the captured ogre magi. "Ur-Krurk's getting food and water."

Either not seeing the difference, or not caring, Jek's shoulders raised and lowered.

Ben wished the orc would stop shrugging.

"He wants the title." Jek knocked on the large belt buckle hidden under Ben's coat, covering his abdomen.

What if I don't have the belt? Ben thought about asking, but decided against it.

Jek went hand over hand on the steering wheel to take the last turn to put them onto the final approach to the main building. Jek said, "You will have a minute to reach an accord of some sort."

The violet neon glow of the Meadows Towing sign bathed the front of the building where distant movement stirred, visible mostly by the shadows they cast. Ben sat up to pay more attention.

"Don't get your hopes up," Jek continued. "If an agreement is not made—which it won't be—he has to present half his forces and then..." The orc shot him a sideways glance. "... it's on."

Ben's Anvilsmith chimed. Though his device's communication had been shut down since they left the festival, they had moved into Tex's range. The robot's chat window popped up. "Here's how things look." A tight overlay of the front building filled the screen. "Blue blip is the Ogre Magi who is challenging you." The screen zoomed out to include the building where green dots lit up in the garage. "Green blips are your blood-oathed orcs." The map zoomed way out to show twenty red dots near the front of the building with another twenty peppered throughout the first dozen rows of compacted and stacked cars. They flashed. "These are his guys." The latter twenty flashed. "These guys might have moved from where I've plotted them."

Estimating forty opponents, Ben angled his screen toward Jek and waved his finger around the mass of red dots. "Are these all of his fighters?"

"No!" Jek's head could not have shaken faster if he were a freshly knocked bobble-head. "That's just his traveling guard. He has hundreds, if not a thousand, warriors under his homeland banner. If he had known he was coming to battle, he would have brought all of them." Jek looked at Ben. "There's a general presumption about your kind. So, he'd rather fight now than go home and return with his full army."

"Huh?" The mention of race got Ben's notice.

Jek returned his attention forward.

Ben asked, "Why use forty instead of a thousand?"

Jek's lips twisted in consideration before explaining. "If he gave you time, you'd probably play the human-card."

Ben arced an eyebrow at the orc.

"You know." Jek switched to guiding the steering wheel with his knees. "Call on your kind to," Jek's voice rose in pitch and wavered in fake fear as he flailed his arms. *"Repel the monstrous invasion."*

The imitation made Ben chuckle a bit. He asked, "Is that what we sound like to you?"

Jek grinned with a hint of guilt clinging to his shrug. "Are you saying it's not true?"

"Only if..." Ben exhaled his regret and slumped into the chair. The springs pressed back against him through the thin cushion. "I wish." He had wanted to contact the school, but his Anvilsmith's communication relay had gone on the fritz shortly after he reached Tex. *Just like on the night of Pepperjacks' burning.* Ben's fist balled when he thought about Collins shutting down his ability to contact the outside world. It had to be Collins. *Can't just be a coincidence that it would happen again, tonight, after his Nilosian-ink-eye thing happened.*

The ogre's teal skin could be made out in the distance. Ben asked, "Do I have to uphold any traditions?"

"Nope." Jek remained still. "Just show that you have the belt."

Though the orc had already verified the trophy lay under his coat, Ben decided to try for a loophole. "And what if I don't have it?" Ben had gotten used to Bastion's swirling when it shifted directions and made his head dip. *Stop it!*

A confused frown wrinkled Jek's brow. "But you do have it."

"Let me try putting it a different way." Feeling that he could taste victory just on the other side of his question, Ben licked his lips. "What if I didn't have it when I meet with the ogre?"

"Ohhh..." Catching on, Jek nodded with something close to pride at Ben's being sneaky.

Ben started to nod with him and let a sly smile spread his lips. "Now you're getting it."

"Well, in that case..." Going along with the scenario Jek continued his conspiring nod for a second before shrugging. "Then they'll murder you, your orcs, and ransack the place searching for the belt."

Stunned at the reversal, Ben mouth's popped open, and worked silently before he managed to squeak, "What?"

"Yeah." Jek returned to nodding. "Didn't think you'd think of that, but the ogre could get the title that way, too."

Chapter Seventeen

CORNERMAN

As Jek drove the truck toward the clearing in front of the main building, the blue and red dots on Ben's display scattered. His gaze went from the three green blips on his device to where his orcs would be in real space. All alive in their white Meadows Towing tees, blue jeans, and the black steel-toe Tore Vex boots he got them for Samhain. Their dark green faces framed in relief, they got to their feet and pounded their chest at him

Ben pounded his back. Their thorough elation at seeing him put a nagging suspicion into words. Ben narrowed his eyes and asked, "Jek, why didn't you say, *kill us*?"

"I'm not blood bound, and I fetched you." Jek gave a lopsided grin as he drove them around back. "As long as I stay out of the way, I live."

Betrayal flashed through him. Ben wanted to hit the orc to use their way of showing how angry he'd become. Instead, he hammer-fisted the dashboard. It rattled. The glove box popped open and slapped his knees. Ben slammed it shut. "You son of a bitch!"

"Hey! I want you to win. That party you threw us was great and my brood liked the extra day you gave us for home-time." Jek drove past the other four tow trucks and pulled into a spot. "Trust me when I say that I've had enough of ogre overlords, but..." A helplessness clung to his shrug. "I have to watch out for my hide."

If Ben had done anything like the dashboard punch in the company of schoolmates, Adept Matton would hunt him down to drag him to detention. Ben exhaled hard to get himself under control again. *You slimy snake.* "And to think, I was starting to like you." Ben kept his eyes on Jek through the windows as they got out. The back of the building always smelled from the barrels of used motor oil. *I should punish him ogre-style and make him drink one.* "Unhook my car."

Jek didn't. Instead he took five long strides to get in front of Ben and started whispering as they walked.

Planning to use the car to get away, Ben stopped and pointed at his Transcend raised up onto its rear tires. Some of the orc's words registered.

"... which is why your best tactic is to show how powerful you are at the end of the accord phase." Jek opened the door and entered.

Ben followed. Because of the oil barrels, his mind went back to how a rancid meat and rotted cheese smell used to dominate the building. Now it smelled of Twilight Spring air fresheners.

Jek continued, "Though he won't be phased, it would give some of his forces pause because they know that the first ones in are bound to fall to your might, and—when not defending home-land—no orc wants to die that way."

My might? A deprecating laugh waved up from Ben's stomach as they passed the big-screen TV. *It took me and Bastion together to beat his dad alone.* With his car still hooked, Ben's plan to give his orcs a minute's head start on getting out of here remained the same. For him, though, he'd have to cast *Usain* to escape. A good alternative plan, he nodded. *As long as I don't stop, I should be able to make it to the gate before the Komir amulet runs out of shielding.* Concerned about his companion, his mental checklist spilled through his lips, "No, we're good. I already had Tex sneak out."

Jek stopped and faced him.

Regret snapped Ben's lips together. He pressed them tight.

Bastion's hurricane swirling picked up speed filling Ben's ears with an ever-so-slight whooshing sound.

Jek's eyes narrowed in calculation. From that one sentence, the orc pieced enough together to ask, "You're going to run?"

Ben hated the hopeless shrug that rocked his shoulders. "I don't see this going my way."

Jek tensed, bore his teeth, and balled his fist.

Ben stepped back. He slipped a finger onto his *Orion* spellcard.

Words weighted with anger or disappointment— perhaps both—spilled through the tiny gaps around the tusks in the large pointy ivory bear trap the orc had for teeth. "Put your ring on. Show him that you took out his flesh-father."

Ben retrieved the ring from the bottom of his coat pocket and slid the band warmed by his body heat onto his thumb. *Perhaps I could bluff my way out of this. Play the, look-what-I-did-to-your-dad card.*

Jek reached behind the television and pulled out a baton. The orc pounded its chest in pride before extending it. "How about now, Might-Fist?"

Ben jumped back. "That's a— Where'd you get—" His mind's eye recalled the baton flipping end over end from the Imprisoning Orb as it spat out Ur-Krurk's possessions. "That's... it can't be... that's a Primary's Battle Baton."

Jek stepped closer. "And it's yours."

"Ut-uh." Ben shook his head and slid further back than Jek had advanced. "It belongs to its rightful owner."

Extending it behind him, Jek twisted and hocked it right at Ben's face.

Ben had already ducked. Yet, the ring raised his hand. The rod slapped into his palm and his fingers closed around it.

"You killed the rightful owner." Jek tucked his shirt in. "So ownership transferred."

Ben opened his mouth to correct Jek, again, about Ur-Krurk not being dead, but imprisoned, when a mystic bonding—*it is mine*—relayed the magic stored within the weapon. As though he were holding programmed spellcards, the baton enabled him to cast Magic Volley, Fireball, Righteousness, and Degenerative Aura. *No one passes Spell P III without being able to code Magic Volley and everyone knows about Fireball, but what in the heck are the last two?*

The rod would appear in his hand, when he willed it, and it enabled him to substitute acid for any element he cast, transmuting the stored Fireballs into Acidballs. Amazed, Ben's voice took on a husky waver as he spoke through his inhale, "Wow."

"Yes. And it's yours. Use it." Jek turned and to walk back out. "If a loss is inevitable, I'll have your car loose."

How could an Ogre Magi be a Primary? Studying the dull steel rod—*it's weightless*—Ben waved it back and forth as the Vibrosian Magistrate had at the festival. Where the tip of hers had turned orange, his turned black. *No, it's absorbing light. Wait, it's not light, it's ambient arcane power.*

With the influx of Nilosian energy through the baton, Bastion's swirling intensified. The pressured building within played with Ben's inner ears and made him rock slightly.

Ben stopped waving the baton and tucked it into his belt against the small of his back. Remembering an off-hand comment Adept Love had made about battling regenerators in the few days of *Dueling* class he'd attended before his parents pulled him out, the baton probably didn't belong to the Krotosian. *The weapon couldn't have belonged to Ur-Krurk. The acidic focus means it's supposed to combat regenerators like Ogre Magi. If someone disarmed him, they'd be able use his baton against him with devastating results.* Ben exhaled. *Then who did it belong to?*

Ben pushed the thought from his head as he went to the kitchen. Filling the air better than a freshener, a large pot of barbeque sauce had boiled over and splattered on the stovetop. He turned off the burner and looked out the window to see the Ogre Magi's forces.

Orcs wearing a style of studded, black leather armor he had only seen on the other side, had come out of hiding and now were bumping into one another, hyping-up for the coming battle.

The Nilosian energy in his head stilled. Bastion began soaking it up like one of those flat sponges that grows in size as it takes in moisture.

The beast really wanted out to go at the ogre and, for a moment, Ben considered giving in to let it loose. He mumbled to the window, "Where's the ogre?" He pulled his Anvilsmith and flipped the switch to make it voice-activated. "Ping. Set mode to silent. Ping. Record." He holstered it back on his hip and took a deep breath. "Ping. Vibrate after one minute."

Ben stepped into the work bays. Still considering a hasty retreat, he whispered as loud as he dared to his orcs, "Guys. Go."

They nodded. Toad was first into the kitchen. The other two followed. About to go back in himself, a deep, growling voice yelled, "I challenge for Might-Fist!"

The belt buckle against Ben's abdomen thrummed, pulling Ben's recollection of Ur-Krurk's defeat. *I did beat his father.* The idea of fleeing switched to the back burner as a desire to keep the belt—if not the title—took the spotlight. *Let's see how this goes.*

Gassed up, Ben turned to face the ogre.

Chapter Eighteen

TITLE FIGHT

A STEADY CALM filled Ben where fear and dread had been building during the drive to Meadows Towing. The rubber-oil smell of mechanic work filled the five work bays and, looking out the bays at the score of hunter-green orcs—*pure warrior breed*—in black, studded armor, Ben realized just how ridiculous he must have looked a month ago when he came to reclaim the Node Key with only two conjured gorillas. He, Abe, and Oscar had run from the last row of stacked cars a hundred feet away and got caught in the open. Right where the orcs stood.

A barking laugh came from above them and the ogre clad only in a loincloth—*he's a deeper teal than his father, wonder what that means*—floated down to stand before the orcs. Like his father, Ur-Krurk's son possessed a massive upper body set on a long torso that made up two-thirds of the monster's height. Unlike his father, the stunted legs were powerfully built. Totally discounting

Ben, the ogre magi turned and spoke in a rumbling growl to his men.

Ben had been practicing the Giant tongue with Jek, but the ogre's words were too swift for his rudimentary grasp of the language.

The ogre stopped mid-sentence to laugh harder. His wide, powerful shoulders rocked up and down beneath a large bauble of top-knotted black hair.

The mirth jumped to the orcs who howled along with their master.

Waving at Ben with a massive, clawed hand, the ogre uttered another rapid string of sentences.

Before they could rekindle their spat of laughing at him again, Ben raised his chin. "Dare to say that in English?"

The orcs stopped laughing.

The ogre's shoulders stilled as he turned. His glowering violet irises fixed on Ben from the pitch-black orbs. English, vowels too short, consonants too hard, slopped out, "I say, 'You aren't ev'n a full-grow.'" It snarled, showing a mouthful of sharp tar-black teeth. The ogre continued, "I also say, 'Had I know my flesh-fath'r had grow so weak, I would've dethron'd him months ago."

Bastion threw itself at Ben's sinuses.

It stung. *What's it doing?* Ben eyes watered a bit. He rubbed them. "Leave my property now, and you get to live."

The ogre laughed again. In a near fit, he leaned his head back, and struggled to speak Giant while pointing at Ben. When he finished, his orcs joined in.

Hooting, they mirrored their master and kicked their heads back in laughter.

Ben's Anvilsmith started to vibrate down the last few remaining seconds of the minute timer. Remembering the small gap of time between when he set the timer, spoke to his orcs, and then faced the ogre, Ben slid his hand to his hip. Touching his *Orion* spellcard, he channeled as much energy into it as he could. Five reds bursts flashed before him as his gorillas materialized. Three of them were empty-handed, one —*Abe*—had two knives and—*Oscar*—held a greatsword.

The ogre's laughs eased as he spoke Giant. This time, Ben recognized the last word and translated in his head. *Argosian*.

"I'm not an Argosian!" Ben threw his coat open.

The ogre's gaze fell upon the belt and darted to the Primary Rod as Ben waved it in a low, rising arc.

A tenebrous sigil at the tip of his baton drew light in and formed a symbol similar to the ones Ben had seen in the book Elder Komir gave him.

All laughter stopped. The ogre paled to a powder blue. The closer of his warriors took a step back. Two dog-headed monster-men stepped out of their hiding place behind the first row and began to slink away.

In his head, Bastion roared.

A slight growl rolled from the base of Ben's throat. He focused on the ogre. "Yeah, this is what you face." Ben waved the rod again. The tip absorbed enough surrounding light to obscure the symbols and noticeably dim the area for fifty feet around him. "This is Meadows Towing and I—"

Before he could finish declaring himself the Might-Fist, Bastion threw itself at his eyes again.

Ow! Ben bit his lip as the blow made him lean forward.

The ogre flinched and the front row of orcs took a stepped back.

If they had been on the playground of Ben's elementary, prior to the Arcane Primary Academy, he would have given each of them two punches on the arm for punking. His Anvilsmith stopped vibrating. The minute had expired.

None of the ogre's forces advanced.

Bastion whipped the Nilosian energy in his head into a roaring whirlpool.

Ben almost swooned. His head rolled around his neck.

Bastion doubled in strength. The beast inside pounded at Ben's skull to get out at the ogre.

What are you doing? I can't fight you and him! Ben struggled to complete his earlier sentence.

One of the ogre's orcs took a tentative step toward him.

Ben's conjurations inched toward the enemies and pulled at the far range of their bounds. He only had to let them go and it would be on, but there was still a chance he could bluff the ogre and end this without any bloodshed.

Bastion roared again.

Instead of words, another growl came from Ben's throat. *What the—*

Bastion hammered harder.

Ben found his arm waving the baton of its own accord. Nilosian energy jumped from the tip, unbidden, to the five crimson gorillas. They grew four feet taller, their skin turned back and their hair darkened a ruddy brown. Their torso elongated and sprouted a secondary set of arms.

They've become whatever Bastion is.

More dog-men came from hiding at the rear of the ogre's wide-eyed forces and slid away.

Only the black-clad orcs stood their ground with the ogre. From deeper in the scrapyard, two large, gangly forms stalked through the shadows, drawing closer to the pending combat. They paused for a moment at the corner when they saw the five, nine-foot-tall, four-armed gorillas, then continued—with wide, blood-thirsty grins—into the violet light cast by the Meadow's Towing sign. Two nasty green tuzvuls, arms, nose, and ears stretched to nearly twice normal length—*just like in my books*—moved to the ogre's side. Fearless and ready for combat, they flanked the ogre.

Ben tried to direct the Nilosian energy into the Degenerative Aura spell.

As the energy swelled to his command, Bastion lunged again and again. The baton throbbed hard with each blow from the beast against his skull.

Stop! Ben stumbled forward. *It!*

The ogre flashed a jagged, ferocious grin to match his tuzvuls. Between the tuzvuls coming forward and Ben's erratic movements from refusing to let Bastion out, the orcs' fear abated.

Ben opened his mouth to tell them to stop.

Instead of words, a furious growl ripped up his throat.

Ben's vision through his own eyes—*what's going on?*—became disjointed. Distant. Limited. It was as though his awareness had been yanked backward in his own mind.

Bastion flung his consciousness aside and seized control of his body.

Dislodged in his own head, Ben splashed down in the swirling, ice cold Nilosian energy. *Ah! Freezing!* The dark power rolled his awareness around his skull like a leaf in a flash flood of black ink.

A distant familiarity—*Bastion's talking?*—worked his throat and vocal chords. The words that came were in perfect Giant. "I am Bastion!"

From inside his head, Ben could understand, perfectly, what was being said. Though he never spoke with Bastion, his suspicion about the beast had just been confirmed. *I knew he could understand me!* An icy undercurrent pulled Ben under again. He stroked hard against it to get back above the surface.

Bastion continued to work his throat. "I am your Might-Fist!"

As though disconnected, or coming out from under anesthesia, Ben's arm moved as Bastion waved the baton back and forth. The subzero black power in his skull around him began to rise higher.

The undercurrent yanked again.

Uh! No! Ben's strength waned.

Like looking through the wrong end of a telescope, Ben saw his hand through his own eyes. *Still human. He didn't transform.* Arcing the ebony rod in a slow, all-encompassing arc, his skull neared capacity.

"Now." Bastion said, "It's just a matter of how many die before the rest of you realize it." The beast in his body channeled Nilosian energy into the baton.

Ben's consciousness swam away.

Chapter Nineteen

VEGAS AFTER DARK

A SOFT LIGHT worked at the darkness. Though groggy—
I'm alive—Ben's brain dumped a sense of euphoria into
his sleepy bloodstream, putting his dim awareness on a
faster track to recovery. After Bastion's betrayal, he
wasn't about to take his return to consciousness for
granted. The smell of sautéing onions filled the room.

Thank goodness. It was a nightmare. Ben exhaled and
relief spread through him. *Mmm, wonder what mom's
making. Hopefully omelets.* He rolled his head back into
the pillow, took a deep breath of the intoxicating scent,
and let it out.

Wait a minute.

Between the lack of sound from any of his family's
televisions and the feeling of furs beneath him, a
chilling reality—a reality he couldn't escape—settled
upon him. *I'm not at home. I'm...*

Hoping against hope he would be wrong, Ben
opened his eyes.

An eight foot by six-foot Crystal Waterfall Scrycell

viewing glass covered most of the opposite wall. Gazing upon the inactive mystic viewing device—the largest he had ever seen anywhere—Ben heard his worried gulp. His gaze went to the spot on the beige shag carpet where he had first gotten a good look at Ur-Krurk standing with a turkey leg in one hand and a sword in the other. Besides the carpet and the room being clean, nothing had changed since Ben had stolen Penelope away from here.

Shit.

Ben had offered the room to the orcs, but each insisted that he, the Might-Fist of Meadows Towing, should keep the room. *Shame I never stayed here overnight.* His gaze went to the rungs he had installed above the headboard to get to the roof access latch in the Plexiglas ceiling. The support beams were also Plexiglas. *Talk about a gorgeous view of the sky.* The part of his brain that registered his situation tried—and failed —to derail his appreciation of the moment. *Waking up here's not bad. No alarm clocks and no knocks at the door to get me up for chores. Just an easygoing rouse by natural lighting.*

Like a bashful cat, the rising sun peaked over the wall spilling direct sunlight on him. Ben closed his eyes, sighed, and went to rub the weariness from his face. A length of chain rattled as his arm stopped six inches from the bed. The halt came from something wrapped around his wrist. When he pulled a bit harder, a similar bind on his other wrist pulled his arm into the mattress. "What the—"

He opened his eyes and tried to lift his head. A band pulled on his forehead. The further he lifted his head from the pillow, the greater the resistance became. Except for his coat—*the belt's gone too*—he still wore his school uniform dress shirt, red tie, and slacks. *Better than being naked.* He exhaled and tried not to think what being stripped would have meant. *Much better.*

Ben strained to hold his head up a bit longer to see his wrists. Each had one of those tanned, stiff leather, hospital-grade restraining cuffs. He lifted a leg—*where are my shoes? Where are my socks?*—to see a similar cuff on his ankle that pulled his other leg into the bed if he lifted it too high. *Oh shit, shit.*

His neck gave from the strain.

Ben's head fell back into the pillow. He opened his mouth to call out to his orcs and stopped. *From the setup, Bastion obviously lost. If I call out, my captors would know I'm awake and, doubtlessly, start a long series of torture sessions.*

Too clearly he recalled Penelope covering up the horribly split bruises on her face with the mess of her blood-matted hair.

Ben closed his eyes. He tried not to think of the ogre flaying his skin, strip by strip, to flash-fry his flesh before eating each slowly as though enjoying a rare delicacy. *Uhh.* Ben rolled the words over in his mind. *Rare. Delicacy.* His stomach took a tumble as the month old memory of the ghastly, maggot-infested gray meat that hung from a hook in the living room came to mind. Since taking over, he had the meat trashed and a heavy bag suspended from the hook, but the bag could easily be taken down to hang him like that last living thing that had graced the hook.

A section of the gray decaying meat on a nearly

unidentifiable ribcage flash before his mind's eye. Countless wriggling maggots were going to town.

His throat constricted and his stomach burbled a queasy rumble.

Shaking his head against the images, Ben's imagination started to spiral into the different tortures that he would be subjected to. His thoughts froze. *What if Jek told them about Ur-Krurk not being dead, but captured in the Imprisoning Orb.* Ben gulped again. *He'll probably free his father and put me in. If I'm lucky, in the short run, they'll see what starvation and loneliness does to me.*

Soft padding, like a dog, sounded on the stairs.

Trying to appear like he was still unconscious, Ben closed his eyes lightly. He focused his will on being non-responsive to whatever stimuli they tried.

Two high voices whispered to one another as they entered the room. The language they were speaking had rolling vowel sounds with a guttural, Orcish edge to the consonants. Dragging sounds came from the wall to tap against the footboard of the bed.

Steady breaths, Ben. Keep 'em steady.

Like when his youngest brother would walk on his bed, pressure sank into the mattress near his right leg. Another mattress dip joined the first. They walked along his body and stopped at his torso. Whispering in the unknown language, one of them poked a narrow finger with a ragged fingernail into his stomach.

Ben didn't react.

His belly gurgled and churned. A strong oniony burp rolled up his throat and puffed through his lips. *Uhh, what the heck is that nasty taste?* Something horrid— barely masked by the strong onion flavor—bubbled his guts. *What in Hell did Bastion eat?* He wanted to suck the rank tang from his mouth and spit. *Whatever it was, it must've been, rubbed with onions, stuffed with onions, served with onions, and he must've had a nice oniony soda to wash it down.* Another burp passed through him. *How repugnant.*

They exchanged a volley of whispers before a narrow finger, without a notable nail poked into his other side. His gut gurgled again. The creatures brought a strong antiseptic smell with them.

They probably want to make sure I don't die from infection or bed rot before I could be thoroughly tortured.

The two started whispering again as they walked down toward his feet.

Please don't poke my feet.

Pressure on the mattress left from his left side, followed by the other. A short dragging sound started before a smack slapped from beyond the foot of the bed. A word, sharper and louder than any prior, whipped out like an aftershock. The short dragging ended with another tap on the footboard.

Crap, they're coming back.

Padding sounds shuffled through the shag carpet toward the door.

Ben dared to sneak a peek. About three feet tall, he noted their long thick-peaked ears, baldheads and gnarled skin. *Goblins...* His breath hitched in his chest. In the chapbook—*Grotesque Goblinoids*—handed out in the first week of *Mythic Monsters I* for home study, Goblins were supposedly the second smallest of the goblinoids, the most plentiful, and the most insidious of crafters. His former concern for what the ogre's brutish wrath may hold paled to the unknown torment the goblins could manufacture... Especially in a scrapyard.

The lead goblin's mottled, yellow-green skin had patches of deep green, like lush sprigs in a field of dying grass. The other was a calico of browns, tans, and black. Both wore yellow dish gloves and black rubber aprons which didn't fully wrap around their bodies, leaving their bottoms bare like hospital gowns. The calico smacked the back of the other's head, muttered, and closed the door as they left the room.

Ben waited five seconds to give the goblins time to get down the stairs. Then, taking the size their ears into consideration, he gave them another five. Taxing his neck muscles again, Ben lifted his head to scan for a means of escape.

Ur-Krurk's greatsword, a massive claymore with a human-sized metal skull where the blade went into the hilt and tiny skulls on the pommel and cross-guard—which Ben had stashed away in the basement—sat, tip down, behind the door. His coat hung from the right skull. The closet lay open. The spare set of clothes he had put there a month ago were still neatly folded on his Zephyr board on the top shelf. A tiny mechanical frog, Kermit—his first companion—sat idle next to the Zephyr's upturned rear.

Ben had been saving his allowance to buy the module which would make Kermit voice-activated, but he had forgotten the plan shortly after getting Remy. He sighed. The sigh weighed with all of his disappointment at how quickly he'd tossed aside the plan when a better companion had come along, and then again when he got Tex.

His neck muscles began to ache.

No companion. No tablet. Ben eyed the slight gap between Kermit and the Zephyr board where the formerly cursed Anvilsmith tablet used to sit. *If only I hadn't moved it to my budding basement laboratory...*

Though stuck for a solution, Ben refused to give up. *Gotta unscrew yourself. Clear your mind. You're missing something simple.* He eased his head back to the pillow and thought, and thought, and thought.

Chapter Twenty

COMPANION TROUBLE

As THE SUN rose higher in the sky, the slat of sunlight that had rested on Ben's face traveled down his body to just above his waist. If he were not held captive, he would have enjoyed basking in the warm rays. *There's just something about being bound against your will that saps the joy from things.* Though he couldn't bask in the humor, he allowed himself a quick, wry smile. His gaze went to the thick Plexiglas crossbeam under the Plexiglas roof. The smile faded. *When the sun hits it, will it cook me like an ant under a magnifying glass?*

The sustained quiet also weighed on his mind. It was as though he'd gone camping and had woke up before everyone else in the campground. The more he thought about it, the more certain he became that he had read about goblinoids having a tendency to be nocturnal. Then again, how much that certainty came through overthinking it? True, everything remained quiet, but how long would that last?

Only his steady heartbeat thumped softly in his ears.

The silence lay complete and undisturbed over Meadows Towing.

In the silence—

Ben's hand gripped tight. His subconscious held on to the word for dear life. *Silence...* Consciously, he latched onto the word. *There's something there...* He turned the word over in his mind. Nothing. He went to the root. *Silent...* Ben clenched his fist tighter. *Yes!* He had set his tablet to be silent and voice activated. *I didn't use it to cast spells so they may not have taken it.*

Swallowing his spit to wet his throat, Ben called in a low whisper, "Ping." In his predicament, in the silence, his whisper felt like a jungle call. He pressed his lips together and strained his ears. No padding. No goblins. He continued, "Set volume to one."

No sound come up the stairs, but what came was coming up made him salivate. He swallowed again. Seasoning had been added to the onions to caramelize. Normally one of his favorite toppings on a burger, Ben's appetite died and goose bumps rose. *They're probably going to use me as the burger meat. I hope my orcs refuse to eat me.* He frowned at the silliness of the thought and sighed. The Orcish language had specific terms for types of cannibalism. *If they'd eat each other—and they do —they'd eat me.*

Ben lifted his head and turned his face to the coat. Neck outstretched against the restraint band, he hoped the victors didn't know the importance of his tech. "Ping."

A soft ping sounded from his coat. *Thank goodness!* Excitement ripped through him at the sweetest sound he'd heard since Adept Matton had rang the tiny bell to signal Ben passing *Courtmanship IV*.

He rolled his head to the side, a less taxing activity, and spoke toward his coat. "Ping Tex." A faint green light came from the inner folds. Ben smiled at it and relaxed his neck. *Only a matter of time before I hear that sweet synthesized voice. Well, not so sweet. Since the reset, Texas had lost all sense of intonation, but—still—one step closer to sweet freedom.*

Tex said, "Yes, Ben?"

The metallic echo had never been more welcomed. Ben eased out a calming breath. *Stay cool. There's a way out of this mess.* He formed a command stack. "Tex, return to the scrapyard, bring something sharp enough to cut hard leather—"

"Cannot," Tex interrupted.

Forgetting his belabored neck, Ben lifted his head momentarily, looking at the light in his coat as though he were looking directly at Tex and the companion could see his incredulous expression. The resistance on the band pulled his head back to the pillow. "Um, Tex, why not?"

"You gave me specific orders to go home, plug in, and wait for your return."

A quiver—fear, fear of his setting Tex on robot-mode after the pain of losing his companion, fear of the robot-mode's logic being bound to a strict adherence to linear commands—worked into Ben's voice. "Tex, I'm giving you new orders."

"Copy," Tex said. "I am listening."

"Okay." An old superstition ingrained by his father made Ben cross his fingers with hope. "Unplug and return to the scrapyard. Make sure you bring a tool to cut hard leather that is both quiet and something you can use as I cannot move my arms." Ben paused.

"Noted." Tex replied and added, "New commands acknowledged and placed on the stack of tasks for processing after you return. Is there anything else you would like to add?"

Ben's teeth ground. He constricted his throat to keep from bellowing his frustration and resisted the horrible desire to slam his fist into the bed. *That would make the chains rattle and that would call the goblins.* "Fine!" Ben nearly spat out the word. He bit his lip and took a moment to listen for anything on the stairs. *Nothing.* He continued, "Resume the earlier plug in and power back down orders."

"Copy. See you when you get here." As ironic as it seemed, Ben missed the life the old Tex breathed into the words. The old Tex would have sounded sleepy, excited, or sardonic—not monotone.

Ben waited ten seconds. Tex's power-down cycle took much less, but he wanted to make sure he didn't speak too soon. He turned his head to the coat again. The folds were dark. *How much battery life is left?* That momentary thought made him wonder if this was only the following morning or if he'd been out longer. *All in due time.* He put the caboose of the train of thought in its proper order of concern. "Ping." The inside of his coat lit green again. "Remy."

Rembrandt's choppy robotic voice replied. "Yes, sire?"

Ben drew a breath to even his tone and moved his

lips precisely, enunciating each syllable. "Remy, go to the mainframe. Once there, back up Tex's data files."

"Yes, sire."

Ben said, "Ping me back when you are done."

"Yes, sire."

Ben waited. Remy was one of the first Golemcasts and even though he had upgraded its skeleton to the 1.21 model, its mobility still remained quite limited. A small smile turned the corner of Ben's mouth as he recalled Remy losing the race he had set up between it and Kermit. *Robotics is growing by leaps and bounds. Wonder what's—*

Metal screeched and groaned in the distance, mangling the former silence.

Startled, Ben shook. Someone had started the compactors. *What are they destroying?* His budding hope took a twisting dip. *Probably my car. None of them can really fit in it.* The full crushing cycle took two minutes. Right behind it, a second compactor, this one to the east and closer cried into life.

A rumbling came from Ben's stomach. This time, nothing had spurred it. The caramelizing onions had become a constant background aroma, he hadn't moved, and his stomach hadn't been poked. *It's almost like something's in there...* As much as he wanted to dismiss the thought as pure fantasy, he did have some kind of alter-ego-beast roosting in his head.

The thought brought his focus to his Nilosian font. He tried to detect Bastion only to find a halfway restored reserve of power.

Remy's monotone voice called, "Texas 2.0 is backed up."

"Okay." Ben licked his lips. "Overwrite the current programming with an install of the last version of Tex 1.0."

Remy did not reply.

Blood pounded in Ben's forehead. *Crap. Is this against some kind of weird companion Prime Directive? Change not thy mechanical kin for that is the realm of Engineers and Programmers?*

"Verifying," Remy said. "The last version of Texas 1.0 is 1.0000021. The current version is 2.0003015. Sire, are you sure you want to revert this Golemcast Robo-Zen 3.14 v2 with thirty cycles to version one?"

Yes. Wait. Recalling how literal Remy had proven to be, Ben considered the question to make sure the robot was going to do exactly what he wanted. *I haven't updated the chassis. Tex would be running the old firmware...* Everything seemed right. "First, Remy, switch the lever between Tex's shoulder blades from robot mode to companion mode.

"Done. The switch has sunk in and a sleeve covers the area. Do you still want to install Texas version 1.0000021?"

That switch going away had flipped Ben out the first time, which was what made the decision to take the deactivated Tex back to the Robo-Zen outlet to have the switch reset that much harder. Having lost the sarcastic, and somewhat scarily independent, companion to fried circuits hurt just like when his parents had their ailing Mr. Whiskers put to sleep. Ben didn't want to go through that again, but he needed help. The kind of help only the first version of Tex seemed capable of giving. Taking a deep inhalation for one last moment of consideration, He closed his eyes and said. "Yes."

"Doing so now, Sire."

"Thank you, Remy." Ben let the deep breath out. "Power Tex up and have him ping when operational."

"Understood, Sire."

More twisting metal—*they're using the southwest compactor? Are they going to try all five?*—cried in the distance while he waited... and waited....

Chapter Twenty-One

GETTING GONE

"BEN." Tex's synthesized voice came through his device. Sort of hollow and flat at first, his companion's voice came alive with a confused flavor. "Why does my clock read thirty days since I was last active?"

"Blessed be." Ben's fist balled, grasping victory. Having never used his mother's term for expressing good fortune, Ben relaxed his hand and steadied his thoughts. *I'm not out yet.* He looked to the inner folds of his coat as though he were looking at his companion. "Tex, I need you to come to Meadows Towing and bring something that you can use to quietly cut through hard leather—"

Tex interrupted, "I'm not finding any places by that name."

Good old, Tex. A fond smile spread Ben's lips. *Not even waiting for the complete order.*

Tex said, "And would you please answer my question?"

Ben said, "Ping my device and—"

His device sounded a soft ding.

Ben figured he didn't have to say the rest, but finished his sentence anyway. "Plot it on your map."

"Done and done. Now, my question?"

"It's a long story, buddy." Ben allowed relief to creep into his voice as hope began to make a slow return. "I will explain everything—and I mean *everything*—just get here as fast and as stealthily as possible." Considering how the two commands might be at odds with each other, Ben clarified. "In fact, if you have to choose, pick stealth over speed."

Tex replied, "Yeah, yeah, got it." In the momentary silence Ben figured Tex had started on the task set before it. The volume on his tablet raised a bit. "Ben, why am I getting readings that there are two Anvilsmiths registered to you?"

Ben uttered a shushing sound. "Tex, I really need us to be as stealthy as possible."

"Got it." Tex had lowered the volume of its voice. "On my way."

The coat went dark.

The sun traveled across the room. The five compactors had each run five times. The goblins—still reeking of antiseptic, still poking him with rubber gloves—had checked on him twice more. Each time, Ben expected them to cut on him or try to smack him awake, but they hadn't.

Dusk began to dim the bright blue sky.

Tex's head poked up from the foot of the bed.

Startled, Ben shook on the furs then frowned into the emerald energy-lit two-inch diameter lenses set in the robot's orbital sockets.

Tex whispered, "Present." Not for the first time, Ben admired the Golemcast builder's work. Except for the lack of any form of artificial flesh, they had crafted the Robo-Zen cover plates to allow the chassis to move just like a person—albeit knee-high. Tex had an Anvilsmith strapped across its back.

Ben hadn't heard any ruffling by his coat. To confirm his suspicion, he whispered, "Is this the one from my lab?"

"Yeah." Tex whispered back. "Sorry it took so long, but I couldn't find anything quiet that could cut leather. I'd need some sort of tiny chainsaw since I probably couldn't summon the force to work proper sheers. Then, as I was coming up the secret passage—"

Secret passage?—

"From the basement, I thought, surely Ben couldn't be overlooking the simplicity of using his *Silence* spell to mute blasting off the restraints." Tex's lens closures wound quickly as the robot closed his iris and opened to simulate a blink at Ben. He then turned around and sat near Ben's hand so he could work the tablet. "I mean, surely not."

Ben echoed "Surely not." As though coming from behind a cloud, the thrill at having his companion back rose from the area where the month-old sting of loss had taken roost.

As Tex sometimes would, it continued digging. "Then I thought, oh, the tablets are probably out of power..."

The extended good-humored mockery brought a grateful smile to Ben lips. If pushed by his companion, he would never admit to enjoying Tex's teasing, yet, a certainty—*the robot must know*—made Ben's smile blossom into a grin.

Ben tapped the blue *Spellbook* icon, the slim question mark for *Illusions*, and then the flat-lined EKG icon—the only *Illusory* spell he'd learned at the APA. *Wonder why they don't teach us to program any of the other illusion-based spells?* Having only created and cast the *Silentball* in *Spell Programming V*, Ben hadn't taken the time to customize the background or cast buttons. *I have to dress this one up some.*

Tex continued, "Then I thought, no, not Ben. He's too thrifty with his arcane watts. Surely the center of my universe would never be so brash as to expend all of the awatts at his disposal. No, the wise shepherd to which, I, only a lamb stumbling through life, look to for direction, protection, and guidance. Surely not…"

Yup, that's the old Tex—he'll keep on until I tell him to be quiet or silence him with the spell. Ben focused the spell on his companion and tapped the generic two-inch wide by one-inch-tall *Cast* icon. Ten of the hundred arcane watts drained away.

Tex raised his hands over his head and clapped. No sound.

Good. Ben tried to whistle. Nothing. *Good. Gotta make the most of these few minutes.*

Ben swiped back to spell types, tapped the dollar sign icon for his conjurations, and tapped the bullet icon for his *Blast* spell. Having cast from his spellcard so often recently, Ben tried to remember why he'd made the background a hammer driving nails into wood. *Later, figure it out later.* Four blasts, a slip of the headband, and a shove from the bed; he stood free.

He collected his coat. Also dangling on the claymore's hilt were his tablet holster and spellcard band. He strapped them on, collected his Zephyr board and Kermit, and slipped on his spare pair of loafers.

Tex motioned him toward the entrance in the bathroom.

I do have to go, but not here. Ben shook his head and pointed to the rungs at the head of the bed—built for him since Ur-Krurk could fly—that would lead to the roof. A more likely reason for Tex signaling him to the bathroom—*the secret passage is probably in there*—occurred to him, but he hoped there would be one more item to collect.

Tex clamped onto his coat.

Ben climbed up to the roof. Once through the door, the neglected metal, rubber, and plastic smell of the scrapyard filled his nose. Just the same—*freedom*—Ben took a deep inhalation of the crisp night air. *So nice.*

Checking for movement on the grounds, Ben peaked over the front. Several groups of three orcs in black armor did rounds on the grounds.

Trying to plot and time their paths, Ben watched.

When he had visited Meadows Towing on the weekends, Ben would retrieve the Imprisoning Orb from the first "O" in the Meadows Towing sign, and set it in front of the television as he pushed a week's worth of food and water into it. His orcs were almost always out on service calls, so getting it, and putting it back so Ur-Krurk could overlook the scrapyard without the orcs knowing where he was imprisoned, had never been a problem.

If he hadn't known what the mystical prison would

do to the captive, Ben would've just buried it out in the desert, but the Orb had imprinted him with the knowledge of what would happen, and he couldn't be that cruel; even to a monster that threatened to make bloodspots of him and his family.

When the break in rotations came, Ben summoned Oscar, had the gorilla retrieve the Orb and come back up. With Tex still on his coat, the three of them made their way across the roof to the back of the building.

Ben peak ever the edge.

His Transcend sat unguarded where it had been towed and released.

Thank goodness. Ben climbed onto Oscar's back. The gorilla climbed them down.

Still under the magical silenced, Ben opened the card door, dropped into his seat and closed the door.

Tex already had his hand in the ignition. The robot turned his arm.

The car vibrated a bit, but made no sound.

Ben dismissed Oscar and, to keep from spitting rocks out behind him, eased away from the building. Once a row away, he jumped on the gas and zoomed toward a side exit.

Two dog-headed men posted there turned around when the gate started to open. They leapt from Ben's path as he escaped into the night.

Chapter Twenty-Two

MESSING WITH TEXAS

AFTER STASHING the Imprisoning Orb in his *Courtmanship* locker and retrieving the Nod Key, Ben scanned the long, narrow Archon Private Academy's student parking lot. His Transcend remained parked in the choice spot closest to the school doors, where the one-way U-turn doubled back to the second row and final row. The rest of the lot, empty.

Ben hustled to his car, searched all the way around it to make sure it hadn't been tampered with, and— checking for a tail—turned his gaze to the seemingly endless flow of headlights streaking by as cars whooshed down Tropicana Boulevard. *I wonder what the Mundanes see when they look this way? An abandoned school? An unused business complex? An empty dirt lot?*

Tex knocked on the glass.

Nerves strung tight enough to be strummed, Ben jumped away from the sound. Ready to cast, his fingers lay on his spellcards.

Tex waved.

Ben had grown used to the way the robot-mode Tex stayed right where he left it. He relaxed, opened the car door and plopped into the seat. "I take it the transfer of 2.0's data is complete?"

"Yes. Rooted, and indexed." Dismayed, Tex shook his tiny metal head. "Still can't believe you had me in robot mode for a full eighth of school."

"Look on the bright side." Ben carefully nudged his companion. "You're irreplaceable."

Tex looked toward the opposite car door as through talking to a camera. "And then he tried to flatter me…"

Ben slid his hand into his coat pocket. The old fashioned skeleton-key-shaped Node Key warmed his hand. *I should try to start my car with it.* The thought brought a mostly silly, partly wicked smirk to his mouth. "Tex. Face me, turn off your optics and open your chest compartment."

"Okay." The robot turned. The emerald light left his orbital sockets revealing the semi-reflective surface behind the thick lenses. "Just so you know, I'm hacking my programming to never forgive you if you stick a boiled egg in me."

Ben chuckled. "Wouldn't dream of it."

"Good." A quick series of clicks sounded before the chest cover slid down to Tex's knees.

I was looking all over for these. Ben took out his spare set of house and car keys. *Totally forgot I put them here.* He took the key ring, tossed it in a cup holder and placed the Node Key inside. Ben slid the cover back into place. Clicks locked it in.

Ben said, "Tex, set up a background process with the following specific parameters." He took a moment to organize his thoughts. *Can't believe I'm setting up a contingency plan for if I get killed or snatched up.* "If I go missing, without any form of communication with you for a month and a day, turn the contents stored in your chest over to Master Reynolds."

"Programming now." Tex nodded. "While we wait, could you fill me in on what happened between my backup and…, uh…, me popping my top?"

Ben snapped on his seatbelt, started the car, and flipped the convertible switch to start the slow process of putting the top down. "Okay, let's see… While you were out, we saved an Argosian from a Krotosian. I helped her get home, came back, captured the Krotosian, and recovered the Node Key." While Ben spoke, a wide smile had formed. He'd missed having someone to confide in, and realized just how delighted he was to have the original Tex back. He admired his companion standing there on the center console. *Best part.* Ben stared into the reflective metal behind the lenses. *He won't see this silly-ass smile.* Bringing the smile under modest control, Ben said, "Optics on."

The green energy flicked back on.

Remembering one last thing, Ben jutted a thumb toward the school. "Oh, and the usual drudgery that comes with an eighth of schoolwork."

Tex faced the Archon Private Academy. "So, *Courtmanship V* next eighth, right?"

"Yup." Ben jingled his keys.

Tex turned, slid down the side of the steering wheel, and placed his tiny hand in the ignition before Ben could place the key. The car revved and headlights flashed to life. "Remember, you have to pass to stay on track for the record."

I know, Tex. No pressure, right? Ben nodded.

The robot dropped onto his knee, hopped to the center armrest, and stepped into his safety harness, which resembled the swings at parks for toddlers. Tex hooked the first bungee-strap around his waist to the left. "The registrar codex shows Master Reynolds teaches *Spell P*. Ten and higher." He secured the second bungee strap around his waist to the right, and kicked off to dangle in front of the Transcend's control console. "This means only six more eighths of the draconian Senior Adept."

Ben's eyes widened. His smile broke. The integral part of their relationship—a shared understanding of Collins' trickery—had been lost. He dropped his face to his hands. His forehead tapped the horn.

Tex's tiny hand rested on his leg. "What's wrong?"

Removing his hands, Ben leaned back in his seat. With the top down, he looked at the dark blue sky. Dusk had settled across the Vegas Valley, and only a few stars shone through the city's strong ambient light. For a brief moment, he longed for the view from atop the Suntouched Spire. *Things were simpler over there. No Collins. No Bastion. No ogres and orcs wanting to end your life...*

Tex gave Ben's coat a gentle tug. "Ben?"

Can't tell him straight out. That'd be slandering an Adept and he'd have to report me. Ben rubbed his face. He tried to think of a way to explain what Tex would see as an impossible scenario. "Well." Ben thought a bit longer before he snapped his fingers. *Got it. First the defining difference between him and v2.*

Ben faced his companion. "Okay, so there was a moment when I was going to go after the Krotosian when I wanted you to channel the awatts from one Anvilsmith to the other…"

Tex had already started to shake his head. "Why would you ask that, Ben? You don't have the authority to approve such a waste."

Crap. He won't let me set the premise. With Tex shutting down his hopeful line of recovery, Ben set his mind to finding an alternative, and half-heartedly continued the conversation as he backed out of the parking spot. "I know." He shifted to drive. "However, when I spoke about not wanting to override you, you decided to do it on your own."

"I did?" The slight synthesized reverb in Tex's voice became a bona fide echo and rang for a full second.

Registering the phenomenon, Ben stared at the small robot. While looking at Tex, he missed slowing for a speed bump. The Transcend rocked hard.

"Okay." Tex fell from the armrest and dangled from the bungee cords. The echo gone, his companion asked in his standard, synthesized voice, "Where did I back myself up?"

Ben hit the brakes. "What do you mean?"

Tex swung. "Channeling awatts could have caused me to completely freeze." Tex turned in his harness, put his back to the console, and kicked his legs to continue swinging. "That level of back up is not a part of my standard programming, which is why it takes higher authorization to happen."

Ben shook his head and shifted his foot from the brake to the accelerator. "There was nowhere to back you up. It was just, me, you, the car, and the tablets."

Tex's hand flipped back and he stuck his USB port into the spare Anvilsmith. "There is an archive volume here for Tex 1.0000075, but I don't have rights to it."

Ben slammed on the brakes at the lot exit. "Root the file, and index it. Then reinstall."

Tex bumped against the console. "You do not have the authority to approve said task." The small robot's faceplates shifted away from the center, pulling the bumps he had for cheeks up and back. This turned the small, square speaker to an upward-turned half-moon slit.

Though the joints and plates had always been there, Ben's jaw hinged open with amazement. *He can make expressions? Cool! How many times have I wondered at that deadpan face?*

Tex continued. "You'd have to override."

Chuckling, Ben gave an enthusiastic nod. "Do it."

Tex mirrored the nod. "With pleasure."

Chapter Twenty-Three

PRYING THE THIRD EYE

Ben waited in the parking lot for a few minutes for Tex to reboot before he started to drive around Vegas.

When stopped at a light, with the top down, people looked at Ben as though he were crazy, but the cool October night air, and the wide night sky above, kept his freedom fresh in his mind. The magical knack in his coat—the same as all the other trench coat wearing APA students—would protect him from extreme temperatures. Last Yule, one of the coldest on record, he'd seen other casters' teeth rattle while he barely got goose bumps.

He'd only lost part of one night and day. Ben kept his eyes peeled for the Legerity with the purple rear-end that he'd seen in Papa Mojo's crystal ball. Just as he'd been taken captive, Mojo said Clarissa would be as well. After suffering through the thoughts of what could have happened to himself, Ben would do his best to keep real horrors from being visited upon another…

The light turned green. Ben didn't move his foot to the accelerator.

Car horns blared from behind him. The sound thinned away to nothing as a vision flashed—their Transcends parked on a long, paved road splitting the hardpan, he and Malcolm flinging spells at each other in the desert. They were being watched—and then it faded.

My thinking of people and then they show up... Gary called this a 'third-eye.' Does it mean I have to battle Malcolm to save Clarissa? If so, why wasn't Clarissa in the vision? Was she one of the ones watching us?

Pressing his lips together, Ben muttered, "I have to learn to control this."

Tex stirred. "Control what?"

"Welcome back, buddy!" Ben checked the car clock. *Wow, ten already.* Tex had been idle for nearly three hours. "How'd it go?"

The small robot's face plates shifted to show the slit smile. "I'm back and feeling better than ever!"

Enthusiasm bent Ben's neck. If his stomach hadn't started to gnaw at him, he would have put his hand out to high-five. "So glad to hear it. The other you was..."

Tex's green lenses, and the world around him dimmed.

Another vision—him sitting at an intersection with 24-Seven convenience stores on opposite corners. Malcolm—

A pinch on Ben's pinky snatched him back to reality. He pulled his hand away from Tex and rubbed it. "Ouch!"

"Your eyes went glassy and you're driving." Though the robot could not see the road, Tex pointed forward.

Ben focused forward on the road and dipped his hand into the ashtray for one of the open packs of antacids he'd taken to keeping there. He ripped the pack a bit further, popped two of the chalky discs into his mouth, and began to chew. The hint of almost, but not-quite-there, cherry flavor signaled he'd grabbed the *Acid Aide* package. Chomping the antacids into granules, he placed the pack back in the ashtray.

Tex rummaged through them to read the names, and asked, "What's with these?"

Ben glanced.

Like a trained drug-detecting hound, Tex patiently scanned the back of the antacid packs in the ashtray.

Stopping for a red light, Ben's brow furrowed, he bit his lip, and cradled his abdomen. "My stomach is killing me."

"Well." Tex lifted a package to read the lower bits. "You can take too many—"

An air horn blared from the car next to him.

Ben's insides quivered. The grumbling in his gut almost seemed to bite him before another nasty, oniony burp rolled up his esophagus. His earlier question, while flanked by goblins and bounded to the bed, echoed back. *What in Hell did Bastion eat?*

"How in the Hell did you rate a Transcend, Baby Ben?"

Malcolm. Ben turned to see the Dunn-Blatt with his two cronies from last night. Though the purple paint job and black buffalo detailing made their cars look quite different, they both were the same make and model. *Of course!* Malcolm had little knobs added so, from head-on, he car would look like a low profile approaching buffalo.

Malcolm revved his engine. "Wanna race?"

Though his stomach churned again and he detested the Dunn-Blatt bully, Ben could not help but feel bad for Malcolm. *He really thinks he's hot shit and popular, but the guy in the backseat looks like he wants to bash his head in. Wonder where his drastic need to compete comes from?* Ben shook his head. "Sort of pointless, isn't it?" Ben added, "Since, you know, we have the same car and all."

"It's not about the car, Benny-Boy, it's about the driver!" Malcolm revved again. "Five golds against my hook says I beat you to The Strip!"

Ben felt bile crawling up his throat and forced it back down. "You disgust me."

Malcolm sneered. "What?"

"You're not getting your hook back so easily." Ben paused to burp, and grimace. Just beneath the strong onion mask, he detected the slightest taste of foul meat. "Hooks are only a gold." *Only a gold, it'd take me a year to earn that.* "Just go buy a new one."

"I need that particular one back." Malcolm revved his engine again. "A platinum, then. That's ten to one. Or are you chicken?"

A souped-up engine thundered from beyond the 24-Seven to the right. Ben's eyes sought the noise and spotted the white Legerity with a purple rear-end in the Pinball Hall of Fame's parking lot.

The light turned green. Ben jumped on the accelerator.

Chapter Twenty-Four

CHASING LIGHTS

TIRES PEELED BEHIND HIM. Malcolm zoomed past leaving a wake of noxious white clouds.

Ben held his breath, applied his breaks, and turned into the brightly lit 24-Seven lot.

Tex had pulled his release to shoot from the passenger seat and dangle in front of the control console. "What are you doing, Ben? We had him off the line! We could've won!"

"This isn't about him, Tex." To keep mundanes from having a reason to take further notice him, Ben backed into a parking spot as far away from the gas pumps and entrance to the convenience store. Once folks look away —and he didn't do anything to draw attention to himself—the Mystique would veil him and keep him concealed.

Ben had once gone near a mundane car as it sat at one of the gasoline dispensers. His curiosity about what the liquid did for cars had grown too great. When he got close, the fumes made him feel tipsy and dissuaded him from trying to steal a quick taste. When he had mentioned the experience to Blythe, the Junior Adept told him that mundane vehicles needed gas to run. *How ridiculous,* Ben had said, *What if you're running late for school and the gasoline runs out, or, worse, you wake up to find that it evaporated away while you were sleeping?* Blythe had twisted his lips up tight in shared confusion. There were just some things about mundanes no one could explain.

Two Tanaka Stingers rolled into the Pinball Hall of Fame parking lot. The lowered Japanese imports looked more like rolling lime-and-violet flashlights than cars. *It should be illegal to have that much aftermarket neon.* The two cars each had the same number of lights, but where one had light green, the other had light purple and vice versa. They pulled up to flank the Legerity in the parking lot.

Ben pointed. "It's all about the white one, Tex."

The drivers of the imports got out. *Whoa, they're grown men.* He didn't know thirty-year-olds—or close to —drove those kinds of cars. *They must miss high school.* One of them stuck their hands into the Legerity to shake hands with the unseen driver. *Can't see in. Must be some kind of cloaking magic.* Each of the thirty-year-olds pulled out a wad of mundane money from their jean jackets, folded thick, and passed it in through the Legerity's window. They then rushed back to their cars as thin slits for reverse lights lit up on the Legerity's purple trunk. Rocking with power from each rev of the engine, mufflers gurgling, the American-Steel muscle car slow-rolled—almost strutting with confidence—to the exit and into the center lane on Tropicana.

The two flash-light Tanaka Stingers zipped out to flank the Legerity, the three of them forming a ten-mile-an-hour rolling roadblock. Other cars that were cut off laid on their horns, their drivers cursing and jutting middle fingers out their windows.

Ben also exited the parking lot and wound up stuck in a lane behind three cars with angry drivers. He swerved to the fast lane which only had two.

He gripped the steering wheel and glanced at Tex. "I'm only concerned about keeping up with the white car."

The small robot's facial plates shifted again, this time two plates dropped from the top of his lenses while two rose from the bottom, making the round orbital socket seem to narrow in concentration. "Gotcha."

Don't think I've ever seen a Golemcast do that. Ben's throat pulsed an appreciative, "Hmph."

Abruptly, the three cars burned rubber and sped away. They raced up to Maryland Parkway and made sharp lefts.

Drawing honks and middle fingers of his own, Ben dipped and dodged through the small spaces that opened up when the slower traffic started to pick up speed. He paused at the red light at Maryland for a gap in cross-traffic before making the turn.

Far ahead, the three cars zoomed out to the newer part of McCarran airport.

Lowering his pedal to the floorboard, Ben's needle rotated over one hundred as he kept them in sight. He lost them for a moment on the Russell Road curve, but the light from bright Japanese imports signaled they were racing down Eastern to get on the Beltway heading out to Green Valley.

Thinking about Clarissa, Ben edged his car a little faster to make up some ground before also getting on the expressway. "Give me one of the boosts, Tex." Out of the corner of his eye, Ben noticed Tex punch a code into the console. *If I can learn the codes, I can be the master of my own vehicle.*

"Ready, steady," Tex warned. "Go!"

The boost didn't register on the speedometer.

Ben held the wheel tight and made small moves as Adept Dugan had instructed, keeping control while slaloming through traffic at high speed. The Stingers lights and the Legerity's slits, further down the highway steadily grew larger as he closed on them.

The Legerity led the three vehicles as they banked right into darkness.

Without looking down, Ben tapped *Spells, Enchantments, Elfsight,* and *Cast* on his Anvilsmith. He killed his headlights. As though called down from the sky, ephemeral magical starlight rained on the highway and surrounding area casting a sheen on the dry pavement.

There were knocked over cones at the entrance to the closed Pepcon Obdurium quarry off-ramp. *Crap! There going down into Old Hendo.*

Only recently finding out things like orcs and ogres were real, Ben didn't want to go down there to find out if the horror stories he'd heard about Old Henderson were also true. Almost too late, an image of Clarissa with her pixie-cut blonde hair flashed in his mind's eye.

Ben made the turn.

The dark industrial sprawl that had boomed after the Pepcon discovery rose up to meet the freeway's height as the off-ramp went down, down, down.

Most of the buildings in Old Henderson were at least three stories tall, and all of them had been built with cinder blocks. Age showed in their peeling paint. A hundred feet above street level hovered a thin, smoggy haze. The distance Ben could see with his Elfsight spell dwindled to half.

He slowed down.

The Legerity's rumbles and the Stingers whines were quite audible.

Ben tried to sense the way they went. *Not possible. Too many echoes.* He admitted, "I lost them."

Tex popped above the dashboard and pointed. "Turn right up there."

Ben did. In the dark, his spell turned the neon-lit cars way down the street into beacons of amazing light. "Give me another speed surge, Tex." Not going over a hundred miles an hour this time, Ben tried to spy the code. *Six. One. Something. Nine. Something. Zero.*

Tex pressed the power button on the radio. In five seconds, the Transcend rocketed forward to the same speed as on the freeway. "Only one of those left," Tex said.

"Noted." Ben's knuckles went white on the steering wheel when the two neon cars split up to go in different directions. A glimpse of brake lights signaled the Legerity had turned left. Ben applied the brakes, ending the spell, and swerved to avoid a huge pothole—and an impossibly large postal mailbox on the sidewalk—as he turned onto Dove Boulevard.

The Legerity's taillights were in front of him.

Jumping back on the accelerator, Ben recalled a school field trip a few years ago to the Anvilsmith Industrial Complex at the far end of the ten-lane street. Even at night, the squat dome covering the Pepcon Obdurium deposit stood alone, like a spider in a web of buildings, protecting a meal.

When Ben had closed to fifteen lengths behind the Legerity, it took a sudden right—as though on rails—without tapping the breaks.

Ben slammed on his; almost standing on them. His car didn't stop in time for the turn. He backed up, and looked down the narrow service alley. A wall stood at the end. "How'd it make the turn?"

"Magic." Tex undid his harness.

Recalling what happened at Meadows Towing when Tex started detecting magic too often, Ben placed his companion on the dashboard and warned. "Be careful. You popped doing that."

"Will do," Tex replied. "It turned right before the wall."

Minding his speed at the end, Ben drove down the alley and turned right. "How do you know?"

"I'm able to track the magical trail it's leaving."

Ben nodded and followed Tex's direction.

The robot navigated him through a maze of buildings. A huge perk to getting a Robo-Zen model lay in the fact that it could detect magic. However, track it? *Great, between that and the face plates shifting, now I absolutely* have *to read Tex's manual from cover to cover.*

The Legerity went through the same areas several

times, doubling and tripling back, until Tex finally said, "Sorry, Ben. I lost it."

Ben applied the brakes. "What?"

Tex gave an apologetic bow. "The car is no longer using magic and, as such, I can no longer track it."

"Okay." Ben glanced around the wide back ally with dozens of rolling metal doors leading into rows of conjoined buildings. *If only Papa Mojo had used his crystal ball to show me the actual building.*

Casing off the it-would've-been-nice thought, Ben said, "Then we're right where we're supposed to be." He hoped one of the rolling doors would stand out from the others. None did. He added, "We're here."

Chapter Twenty-Five

ON BEING A BAGMAN

TEX STOOD onto the dashboard and looked around. "*Here* where?"

Ben said, "Hold on." To hide his car, he backed around a corner and into the closes alcove he had seen.

Five large, forest-green industrial-sized dumpsters lined the length of two walls. Centered against the back wall, a cardboard compactor, just a little under half-full. To its left, a pile of compacted cardboard boxes, strapped tight. To its right, pallets. Surprisingly enough, the garbage area only had the faintest whiff of wood and rot. *Guess they don't dump food here often. Well, no food means no rats or pigeons.* In the open air area, Ben looked to the night sky and found the layer of smog still halved the distance of the *Elfsight* spell's raining starlight.

"Okay." Ben looked to Tex. "A diviner said 'when the car lost me,' I would be where I need to be to save Clarissa." He got out, pulled his Anvilsmith, and recast

Elfsight to extend the duration of the spell, then put the tablet back on his hip.

"Who is Clariss—" Tex hopped onto the driver's seat and crossed his arms. "Why don't you have your tablet *in hand*?"

Tapping the SD cardholder on his side, Ben beamed. "I can cast without it."

A FedPS delivery truck gunned past the alcove.

Ben froze.

The engine droned away, idled, and sputtered out. A rolling metal door clattered open.

Tex leapt out of the car.

Ben quietly closed his door and turned. Tex was out of the alcove. By the time Ben stepped from the recess, Tex had already made it to the corner, his little arm waved for Ben to advance.

Ben hurried over and peeked around the corner.

A pale green orc in navy blue work pants and a blue, white, and green FedPS Delivery polo hefted a burlap bag from the back of the cargo truck onto his shoulder. He adjusted the weight and walked into a warehouse.

Having seen a body in a bag before, Ben knew what —*who*—made up the contents.

Two more orcs, the same light green and in similar FedPS Delivery uniforms, came from the cab to unload a few boxes from the back. The first orc came out with a dolly, slipped it under a stack of three two-foot-cubed crates, and wheeled them up a ramp and into the building. The other two did the same. They emptied the back of the truck, which had been full of the two-foot cubed crates.

Ben lost track of which orc had been the one to move

Clarissa. Finally, two of the orcs climbed into the cab, the third clattered the rolling door closed, locked it, and got in the passenger side of the cab. The truck's engine started and they drove away.

After they were gone, Ben asked, "Any magic active over there?"

Tex answered, "We are too far away."

Ben nodded. He scanned the walls for camera mounts and scry sensors. None. He jogged to the large rolling door and looked at Tex expectantly.

The small robot shrugged at him.

Ben pulled his tablet and typed *Any magic auras (possible traps) here?*

Tex sockets twisted for a few seconds and he shook his head. *'No'* appeared after Ben's question mark.

Running his finger along his spellcards to *Orion*, Ben channeled Argosian energy. The red energy flowed through him and flashed into the card. A crimson gorilla materialized.

Bastion's been awfully quiet. Ben reached out to the wellspring of Nilosian energy still at his disposal and found only magic. Bastion, the creature he secretly feared he might be turning into, felt completely absent. Bastion wanted to use Nilosian energy exclusively, and Ben had grown accustomed to the constant struggle to not do so. For once, both of the energies within him were equally at his disposal.

Relief, like a prisoner with a life sentence receiving an instant pardon, relaxed his shoulders. *Free of the beast.* Then his growing smiled faltered and the tension eased back into his back and shoulders. *If Bastion's not here, where is he?*

The ape hooted softly and bumped him.

Ben took a small step back to check out the lock on the door between him and the burlap-sacked Clarissa. Cueing up *Heracles*, he turned to the gorilla. His eyes danced across the many small scars and then to the knives it held. He smiled. *Is this Oscar?*

Returning the recognition, Oscar bobbed his head and made several quick, quiet hoots.

Cool! I'm able to call the same gorillas. Ben aimed at Oscar and pressed *Cast*. The ape's red hair turned green, and its muscles bulged.

Turning to the door, Oscar sniffed the lock before taking hold of it and twisting.

The metal gave a sharp cry.

Ben glanced around for witnesses and found none. When he looked back to his gorilla, he chuckled.

Oscar held the perfectly intact lock. The metal slider the lock had been looped through, hung twisted away from the latch.

Well, at least the lock was worth the money. Ben lifted the door and held it so that it would not spring all the way up. Before he could point, Oscar had scooped up the burlap bag and cradled Clarissa in his arms. *Forgot these apes act before I can really form my orders into thoughts. So much better than Orion.* For a moment Ben felt bad for mentally slandering the conjuration that he used for most of his school chores, but only for a moment.

The Anvilsmith vibrated on his hip.

Ben pulled it and read the message from Tex. *Either the crates themselves are magical or they each contain something magical within.*

Ben's eyebrows tightened as he tried to admonish Tex with a scowl. He closed the door and led Oscar back to his car. In a hurry, Ben leapt over the car door into his seat.

To be as expedient, Oscar went to leap in, too.

Ben dismissed the conjuration before it landed. *That probably would've wrecked my suspension.* The burlap bag flopped down into the backseat.

A soft, drowsy groan. Then soft snoring.

Ben bit his lip. He hadn't thought to have Oscar lay the bag in the back. The inevitable chase Papa Mojo warned about would be starting soon. Ben set Tex in his harness. "Map a way out."

The robot's hand flipped back and he plugged in to the console. An overview map of Old Henderson populated. A white line showed the most direct route through the alleys to Dove Boulevard. To keep the car quiet, Ben drove at a crawl for the first two turns and applied more power as he hit a few straight paths. He opened the rest of the way up when they turned onto Dove.

While they were going up the onramp to the freeway, Tex asked, "What was that look you gave me at the door for?"

Ben checked his rearview mirror. *A dozen headlights, at least.* Minding them for any signs of erratic driving, he scanned the onramp they just came up for more headlights and, in case his expected pursuers didn't have them turned on, for moving shadows. He glanced to Tex. "We are not thieves."

"Oh." Tex looked down for a moment and then motioned his head to the bag in the back seat.

In case some were ahead, Ben returned his eyes to the road. *How can I explain why taking Clarissa—a person Tex doesn't know, from an area neither of us are familiar with —doesn't constitute a theft.* Ben kept his grin locked away. *Ah, Tex, old buddy, this isn't theft. It's kidnapping. Big difference, you know.*

"For the record," Tex swiveled in his harness. "I did not see it as *stealing*. I saw it as taking full advantage of an opportunity."

Though it sounds nicer, that's the same as theft. Ben turned to scold Tex, but the robot's face plates were shifted to pull a single cheek up in a half-smile. Mirroring the smirk, Ben checked his rearview mirror again. No one—as far as he could tell—followed. "Um, we were supposed to be chased."

Tex said, "And you're disappointed because we're not?"

Ben pulled Tex from his harness and set him on the dashboard.

The robot struck a pose to look like an adornment.

"Keep track of the cars behind us, Tex, and let me know if any light with magic or take this exit." Ben took the next off-ramp to Green Valley. This late at night, the street leading to the suburbs had zero traffic. Ben drove past the first two housing communities and asked, "Well?"

Tex looked at him. "I hate to burst your bubble, but we're clear."

Ben drove to a vacant business lot, brought the Transcend to a stop, and—*just in case*—left the engine running. "Well, if we're not being chased, I don't see why I have to speed back to the festival." Grabbing Tex, he held the small robot over the head side of the bag. "Give me a starter snip."

Tex pulled on the burlap with one hand. A slight snick preceded the thin sheet of metal that rotated from his other forearm to extend partway over his fist. With care, the robot drove the tip in while pulling to make the puncture into a small tear. "There you go."

"Thanks." Ben placed Tex on the dashboard and found his tongue wetting his lips in case Clarissa wanted to kiss her appreciation. Though he held onto the hope, he chastised himself. *You've seen too many movies, Ben.* Ripping the bag open, Ben leapt backward to the dashboard and heard Tex slide into the windshield.

Tex chided, "Watch it!"

"That's not Clarissa!" Unabashed, Ben scrambled from the car, slammed the door behind him, and focused on his door handle. His fingers landed on his *Blast*, *Shield*, and *Orion* spellcards. "Is that what I think it is?"

"Hold on." Tex unwedged himself from between the windshield and the dashboard. The robot moved to the edge and hopped down out of view. A moment later, his synthesized voice called out, "Hey, Ben."

Heeding his call, Argosian energy ran down Ben arm and pulsed at his fingertips. "Yeah?"

"What's brownish, has six sets of eyes, and is unconscious in your backseat?"

Just wanting verification that he hadn't lost his grip on reality, Ben didn't appreciate the riddle.

Chapter Twenty-Six

TEX'S RIDDLE

HEARING LIGHT BASS THUMPING, Ben checked over shoulder to make sure a car—particularly the Legerity —hadn't taken the exit. Headlights and taillights flowed on the distant expressway like leaves on a river. A light southbound breeze brought the smell of a fire pit and meat being grilled. A rumbling rocked his gut. Ready for the following bite-back from within his stomach, Ben tightened his abdomen. Nothing. Whatever he'd eaten wasn't getting back at him. Blessedly, he simply had a hunger pang.

Being careful to avoid the parking curb he'd been lucky to miss while scrambling away, Ben eased back to the car to gawk into the backseat. Metallic bronze scales cover its—*her*—skin. The proportions of her face were fairly close to a human's. *Slightly flatter nose, thin lips, a much wider mouth, higher cheekbones...* He studied where the hairline would normally have been and noted the scales became thinner and the flesh bulged to form the base of three fore-snakes. Behind the base of first row of serpents, many more. His eyes tracked one of the snake bodies of the medusa's hair through the rip to see that it ended in a snakehead two knuckles wide.

She whispered, "Don't be startled."

Opposite to the suggestion, Ben reeled back from the car. His finger slapped onto his spellcards and he was as ready as he'd ever been to avoid eye contact. He fixed his eyes on the door handle again. "I don't want to fight you."

Ben tensed at a short tear of burlap. "Good to know because I am at a dis—" Another rip. "Tinct—" The bag tore again. "Disadvantage." Several more short rips came before she gave an exasperated sigh. "Wow, who knew burlap would be so hard to tear?"

A corner of his mouth curled. Not noticing at first, Ben realized he stood a little easier. Remembering how offended Penelope had sounded when he called her *bag-lady*, he remained ready, and asked, "What's your name?"

Another rip. "Alice." And another. "Oh, come on!" Several rapid tears sounded before movement registered in his peripherals as she sat upright.

His eyes rose to see rows of snake bodies lying limp against her back.

She seemed to have more success with quick short tears instead of longer ones. Several more sounded before she turned sideways.

Ben dropped his gaze to the door handle again.

"Seriously," she said. "What is this? Triple stitched?"

Fearing a trick, Ben kept his mirth at her comical intonations from forming a chuckle, but the other corner of his mouth curled, forming a reluctant smile. *Her articulation is amazing. She can't be wild.* Ben asked, "Alice, is there someone you can call for a ride back into town?"

"Why would I do that?" He focused on a snakehead as it rolled forward over her shoulder. "I'm already in a running vehicle."

His index pressed on *Blast*. "It's my car."

"And it's a good one." In the pause, her shoulders shifted and turned. "I've never seen a Transcend in black." She stood in the backseat and his eyes lowered to the handle when he realized she wasn't wearing anything. "Sorry about that, hon." Movement above the door line. "Better?"

Against his better judgment, Ben's gaze rose to see she had the burlap wrapped around her waist. She stepped over the armrest and dropped into the passenger seat with a jiggle.

He lowered his eyes and his cheeks started to heat up. "You're still topless."

Alice laughed. "Well, I have to keep you from accidentally looking into my eyes somehow, don't I?"

Her musical, disarming, and infectious laughter removed his last bit of doubt. Ben found that earlier chuckle rolling from his mouth. His posture had completely relaxed and his fingers were nowhere near his spellcards.

"Seriously, though, this material makes for a lousy dress." Messing with something in her lap, her shoulders moved a few more times. "Perhaps if I'd ripped it better…" She turned toward him and he lowered his eyes. "Hon, listen, I know I owe you for saving me from whomever bagged me and knocked me out. I'm not going to turn you to stone."

Ben scratched his temple. "So, I just avoid eye contact and don't worry about your snake-hair biting me as I drive?"

"Ug!" Alice slapped her hand as though she were smacking sense into him. The muffled sound paled in comparison to a crisp flesh-slap. "I swear, whoever made those damned *Clash of the Titans* movies should have to live in a medusa's body for one year just to see how horribly awkward they've made our lives." A loud thud sounded in his car.

Ben eyes lifted to see she had pounded her fist on the dashboard. "Hey!"

"Sorry. Sorry." She flattened her hand and patted where her fist had struck. "This senseless shit seems so absurdly silly." Her wide, thin lips twisted several times. Part of the turn appeared to be dismay while another part showed pure exasperation. "Sometimes, it really gets to me."

Ben had delayed taking *Mythic Monsters II* and didn't know anything more than what had been presented in the only movie—and its remake—that he'd ever seen with a medusa. Feeling guilty about generalizing based on mundane media, he inched toward the car. "How about you clear up the stereotypes and debunk the myths for me?"

"Love to." Her voice rose with enthusiasm. His eyes went to her hands as she ticked facts on her fingers. "We can totally control the whole flesh-to-stone thing. The serpents are neither hair nor independent. I'm part of a naturally hairless race which, through a curse older and more obscure than vampirism, happens to have a slew of snakes on our heads. We aren't serpent chimerics, like, say, centaurs or satyrs, and, as I am sure you have noticed by how many words I've spoken without a single hiss, we are not sibilant."

She motioned to her mouth with all five fingers, exaggerating her 'esses' to make hissing sounds as she spoke. "Though sssometimesss we ssspeak this way on purpossse." She winked at him as she continued, "Sssince sssome guys love accentsss."

Having accidently made eye contact, Ben started to close the distance. *They're the same bright yellow as Papa Mojo's.* He leaned over the car door and looked closer. A faint filmy texture covered them. "You can see through your eyelids?"

"One, yes." She dropped the accent. "We have two sets." A tight roll of scales above her eyes unrolled. This set of eyelids were a myriad of miniscule yellow scales with a slit of black down the center. Besides the thickness of the pupil, the scales made it look as though she hadn't closed her eyes at all.

Ben waved his hand in front of her face and then leaned back. "So, how long were you awake?"

She raised the outer set.

He flinched, but didn't recoil.

Alice said, "Since you told your car that you guys aren't thieves."

Ben scanned the length of the Transcend. "My car?"

"Yes, very *Knight Rider*. I like it." Alice looked around, motioning to the air, and the completely vacant lot around them. "I mean, who else could you've been talking to?"

"Me." Tex waved. He rolled backward, pivoted, and leapt into the driver's seat to get out of range of the striking snakes.

Alice grabbed a hold of the serpents, which instantly went limp at her touch. "Sorry about that." The scales on her cheeks darkened to a coppery bronze. She looked at Ben with a bashful turn of her head. "It startled me."

Chapter Twenty-Seven

A NEW KIND OF TROUBLE

Between having overbearing parents and going to an all-boys school, Ben hadn't ever really had a completely casual conversation with a girl. At times he thought his parents had conspired to make sure he didn't have a social life where he could meet the opposite gender. After giving it some thought, that absence almost guaranteed him crushing on Penelope or any other girl he got to spend time around. He didn't feel that way about Alice. At least he didn't think he did.

Where the conversation with Penelope had been full of moody, awkward silences—*be fair, Ben. She had just been held prisoner*—the conversation with Alice flowed. Well, it did until he merged into the stream of lights from the whizzing traffic on the expressway taking them away from Old Henderson.

With the top down, the cool night air made a gust in the car and she was leaning forward toward the heater. They had to speak loudly to be able hear one another, but now she yelled, "Look, Ben. I know you think you saved me, but you're wrong!"

Ben arched an eyebrow at her. *So, you typically secure yourself in burlap bags and have orcs render you unconscious before taking you to unknown warehouses?* But sarcasm would get him nowhere. Instead, to try and get her to town faster so he could get back and get Clarissa, he returned his eyes to the road, accelerated, and switched into the fast lane.

"Canyon folk have been going missing since the beginning of the month." She pointed back to the dark industrial sprawl of Old Henderson. "This was the closest I came to seeing where the abductors are taking them."

Sitting on the dashboard, Tex nodded sagely, and added, "What she's saying does make some sense."

Ben shot Tex a look. It said *I've got more than enough dealing with her, so please shut your trap.* Though he had gone through hours of facial expressions so Tex could map them and distinguish under tones, Ben figured he would—eventually—have to actually tell Tex to be quiet.

A plate shifted from the small robot's chin to close its speaker.

Whoa! What the— Ben blinked hard. *He shouldn't—*

Alice wailed, "I smelled one of my sisters there!"

Why didn't she say that earlier? Ben's thoughts bounced back Tex who wasn't supposed to have a chin plate. *All Golemcast have a fixed chuck of metal there. How in the heck did he do that?*

The click of Alice's seatbelt being undone barely registered. Ben glanced over when she stood. The high speeds were making the snakeheads flop. She threatened, "Don't make me jump from this car!"

A bit over-the-top. Not sure how correct he was, Ben said, "Alice, sit down. Your scales aren't armor."

She yelled, "Well, it's either this or turn you to stone!" Fizzles—rainbow light—created an aura around Alice.

Ben frowned at the array of colors and tried to figure out which bands of magic were her primary casting sources. *Can't believe she has that much magic at her disposal...*

Tires screeched. The closer cars behind him swerved away.

Wow, that's not magic. Ben put it together. *It's the Mystique!*

While the Mystique would work to keep her race obscured, It—apparently—could not cover someone standing up in a speeding convertible.

Alice raised a foot to the door.

Does she even know about causing a breach? Wait, does she even know about the Mystique? Knuckles white with frustration, Ben squeezed the steering. "You're going to crack the Mystique!"

Not knowing or not caring, Alice looked out into the night.

Man! Time is shrinking to save Clarissa and now I gotta deal with her? Being known as one of the more obstinate APA students, Ben wasn't used to dealing with someone as strong-willed as himself. "Okay!" He blurted. *Obviously, she doesn't realize the effect she's causing.* Then, in a calm voice. "Okay. Please sit."

As though set to a microphone, the fizzling from the

rainbow aura increased in volume and snapped to throw multi-colored sparks. Worse, the air around her scales began to bulge the aura out forming undulating prismatic tentacles which swished in a meandering fashion toward nearby drivers.

Her passive, I'm-not-playing-chicken, slitted yellow eyes flashed gold when lit by cars on the other side of the expressway.

A rainbow strand curled and whipped at a driver.

The car jammed on its breaks. Skidding and throwing up smoke, its hood dipped.

Holy! Ben slowed, crossed three lanes and took the next off ramp. The further he got from other traffic, the more purposeful the tentacles became. *We're going to flippin' breach!* "Sit! Alice! Please sit!" Fear—fear of breaking all that was sacred to magic-users, fear of being stripped of magic, fear of being forced to live as a mundane knowing a magical world lay just beyond reach—turned his voice into a shrill cry. "Sit! Sit! Sit!"

Jostled and eyes wide, Alice clung to the windshield. She pushed herself down into the seat.

Ben took a sharp right from the ramp onto—*I have no idea what street this is*—whatever and noticed the long wisps of rainbow light around Alice stopped growing. About to exhale his relief—*horror of horrors!*—small, matte gray tendrils extended from the cars that were close to them. Those dull grays reached over the edge of the freeway—*Goodness, what happens if they connect? A breach, that's what. Yeah, but what then?*—from the zooming cars. Ben could swear the occupants up there were looking his way. The Mystique had reached out to them and they were curiously trying to keep an eye on whatever a near-breach made them see.

The colorful and dreary vines came close, but —*blessedly*—did not touch.

Soon, the cars with gray were well on their way further down the freeway and the furthest reaches of Alice's Mystique-enhanced aura began to dissolve into quickly dispersed butterflies, bubbles, and glitter in the Transcend's wake.

A click—*her seatbelt*—came from the passenger seat. Finally able to breathe, Ben drew a deep one, held it, licked his lips, and let it ease out. He pulled over to take another one, and then, a third.

Tetchy, arms crossed over her chest, Alice said, "I'm not getting out."

Chapter Twenty-Eight

ALICE

MY HEART'S THUNDERING. Ben pulled his coat away by the collars to check his chest. The white dress shirt popped away from his body with each beat. *What was it that I read about visible heartbeats?* He tried to recall, but everything not connected to the Mystique, or consequences of a breach of it, flowed through his brain like water through a sock. The thought would hold long enough to register, then be gone when another notion flowed through.

The budding communities of Royal Ridge and Sonoma Springs flanked the road they idled on. From deep in one of them, a group of small dogs started yipping—high points playing against the pounding in his chest and the distant whoosh of traffic. Ben's stomach gurgled unreceptively. From recent habit, Ben popped one of the cherry antacids and chewed the chalky disk. "I said 'okay,' and I stand by my word."

"Great!" Alice's arms unfolded and she turned to face him. "If my sister's not there now, she has been in the last day or so." Almost a separate thought, she sucked a quick, excited breath. "Maybe we can find an office that has an inventory sheet or a manifest."

Ben dragged in one last long, deep breath. Though laced lightly with run-off exhaust from the expressway, it felt like truly fresh air when compared against the haze over Old Henderson. *Amazing how the smog settles over Old Hendo.* Finally, a thought stuck. He took it a step further as his heart stopped its insane mad rapping on his chest. *Almost like the hole the Anvilsmith Dwarves blew into the earth wanted to make amends by sucking away all of the valley's impurities.*

"Alright." *Ready and steady.* Ben started, "So, this might sound personal, but—" He glanced over. Her snakes were still entangled. He gained momentary eye contact before his eyes wavered in their sockets. Losing the fight against the natural urge to see what the serpents—*vipers, definitely some type of vipers*—had been covering, Ben turned his back toward her and tried to make out the graffiti under the white tile on tan stucco Royal Ridge façade.

"Humans." Alice gave an exasperated sigh. Better?"

That was quick. Too quick. He turned. Her hands covered her breasts. "No." Ben said, "That's not what I meant."

Comfortable, she removed her hands.

A part of him—*are the scales of her areola darker? Does she have nipples?*—worked hard at getting his irises to drop below level. Ben brought lessons learned in Adept Matton's *How to Remain Composed Amongst Vixens and Succubi* section of *courtmanship III* into play. His vision stayed above the horizon. Matton's raspy voice—the

Adept had a horrible cold that week—came back to him. "Just think there's no more to them below the chin."

But there is more Alice. Lots of Alice. More Alice than the one set of eyes could take in with a casual glance. Struggling —*get a hold of yourself, Ben*—he asked. "Well, maybe…, could you?"

Alice's yellow eyes kicked up high and rolled away as she sighed and concealed her chest again.

"All right." He could think. He could talk. *A different kind of petrification.* Ben didn't want to smile at the thought, but—since he had kept from perving-out— pride parted his lips to show a sheepish grin. "So, what I was going to ask you is, what color of magic do you use?"

"Magic?" Alice's head pushed back into the seat and the corners of her mouth moved further toward her ears when she pressed her lips together. "Psss, I wish."

Ben started the car. "Being naked—" He cleared his throat and kept his eyes from dropping to the burlap as he made a U-turn and started back toward the onramp that would take them to Old Henderson. "—as you were, how were you going to fight whoever, or whatever, is inside?"

Alice turned in the seat to face him. The slits rose in her yellow eyes, again, and rolled away, again. "Honey, I can turn living creatures to stone."

Waiting for more, hoping for more, Ben checked for traffic at the bottom of the onramp. None. Given how late, and far out they were from the city, he wasn't surprised to only see infrequent streetlights dotting the darkness. Still, he came to a complete stop at the stop sign. His brow furrowed. *So, this is a one-trick pony.* Adept Love had used the term to explain why Jameson Brown never won a top-tier dueling match. The term had bothered Ben because he didn't see that quality in Brown's matches, but Love did.

Finally, he understood what the small Adept meant when he said all of Brown's opponents could see what was coming. *Any thinking person fighting Alice would avoid eye contact, negating her primary strength. Slow down. Maybe she's got some other things going for her. There's more to combat than magic.* Ben meant to ask casually, but the question came out barbed. "So, you're telling me you don't know magic, *and* you don't have any weapons?"

Alice shifted in her seat to face forward. Most of her front snakes slid over her shoulders to cover her.

An involuntary shudder—the thought of a single snake slithering on his skin, from behind his ear and down his neck—shook him.

Serpents coiled in place, Alice dropped her arms. "I didn't say that."

Making a left, Ben drove up the onramp. Taking her back to the warehouse now seemed like just that much more of a bad idea. *Tactics. Talk tactics.* Without a slanderous undertone, he honestly asked, "Then what happens when your stare doesn't work, or, if it works all the time, what about when people are out of range or refuse eye contact?"

She didn't answer.

Has she not given it any thought? Her body's mature. I wonder how old she is.

Before he could ask, she offered, "Part of my

training is being familiar with all sorts of weapons. Weapons I get from opponents."

Ben merged in with the sparse traffic. "Yet you start with none?"

Tex raised a finger like he wanted to say something.

Sorry, buddy, Ben shook his head. *No sniping.*

Jabbing its small metal finger toward Ben's spellcards, Tex lowered his hand.

Ben made a mental note. *Ask Tex about that later.*

"Ugh," Frustration poured from her groan, yet his curiosity had increased with each of her exasperated sighs. Alice said, "Let's just say I'm highly trained for this, okay?"

"*Highly trained*? Like, ready for war?" His eyebrows knitted. Instead of shooting a barbed *I doubt it*, he asked, "How old are you?"

Alice fixed her serpentine eyes upon him. "I'm old enough not to dignify the question with an answer."

His mom had told him never to ask a woman's weight or age. His father had warned if he was ever asked what he thought, he was supposed to always under-guess by ten or twenty percent. It had been one of the few things in his rearing that his parents had been on the same page about.

After a moment, Alice settled into her seat and crossed her arms with no small degree of superiority. She shifted in her seat and flicked his shoulder. "How old are *you*?"

Instead of answering directly, Ben played to his abilities and experience. "I am a caster. I can throw from two types of magic and have over forty spells readily available. Further, I've been training for six years and have been in life-or-death combat." Something close to arrogance building, Ben looked over at her.

Her thin lips were pressed together and rippled with an unmistakably smug smile.

Ben asked, "What? You've fought for your life before?"

She nodded. "Oh yes, a couple of times." Alice pointed to her face. "This is not me doubting your experience." She flicked her index finger away to point back at her expression, "This is me gloating about being older than you."

What a zing and I can't fire back without playing into it. Ben gripped the steering wheel, leaned near it, and ground his teeth. "You know, Alice, I'm really starting to regret not letting you jump."

Alice guffawed, making a sharp sound akin to a snort. Embarrassed at the noise, she covered her bronzing cheeks and continued to laugh.

Ben laughed with her.

Chapter Twenty-Nine

SCOUTING IT OUT

BACKING into the same trash alcove, Ben angled his car in a pool of shadows cast by a sign on top of the warehouse blocking the main floodlight. *That light wasn't on before.* He kept a wary eye out for security guards. An excuse he could tell the guy, if the guard was a guy—*just trying to get lucky*—jumped to his mind and fled—balls to the wall, screaming—at the thought of her snakes reaching out to caress him. Ben could already hear the guard's response if he wasn't human. *Kid, you can't get lucky with a girl you can't look in the eye.*

To test his nerve, Ben wanted to look into Alice's eyes, but—*chicken*—ended up offering, "Tex is great at point."

His companion stood tall. Back ridged, the little golemcast basked in the compliment.

A generator kicked on. The hum honed Ben's attention back on the alcove. *The lack of a powerful odor. That's what's wrong.* For some reason, he had a hard time accepting the garbage area really only possessed a faint rotten smell. If he had time, he'd try to find out why. *The smell should really be stronger.* He put his train of thought back on track. "So, he goes first." Ben motioned to the Anvilsmith. "He relays the layout through my tablet."

Alice extended her hand to touch the Anvilsmith. "Cool! Is this the new—"

Ben smacked her fingertips.

A few of her snakes hissed as, scowling, she brought her hand back.

"It may look like it," Ben explained, "but it's better than any device you've ever seen."

Alice's lips turned in an *oh yeah?* smirk. "Does it have *Kings, Clergy, and Coffers*?"

Ben bit his lip. *That game!* He avoided students at the Academy who played KCC. Most played for real money and he couldn't afford even the smallest of stakes. An alternative iteration *Dragons, Mages, and Magic—same game, really, just rewrapped* proved very popular amongst younger casters. Both versions—all versions—of the game had been forbidden during school hours. There were rumors that the game had even been ported through the Mystique so mundanes could play it on their devices. Only the heavens knew what they call it.

He began to doubt her age again.

"Anyhow!" Ben tapped the dimmed device, tapped *Maps* and *Local*. The Anvilsmith lit showing an overview of the city-sized maze that was Old Henderson. A white line ran from the freeway and ended at a section of a building in the warehouse complex highlighted in red. "You were deposited here."

Tapping a spot on the Anvilsmith, it zoomed into an interior view of the garbage alcove they were in with its wrought iron gates wide open like they were now. "We're here."

Alice looked up, then back at the tablet. "Heh, duh."

"Yeah, duh." Ben didn't want to lose momentum. He pressed *Local* again and the map changed to top-down. Ben spread his fingers and the map zoomed out to encompass only a few hundred feet around the warehouse. "We'll avoid as much opposition as possible, snatch your sister, grab the person I came for, and get out."

"Gotcha." Alice nodded. "Anybody in burlap?"

"No, a particular someone." Ben hadn't thought about coming across other abductees. *Crap!* "Well, I say if they are bagged, we free them."

"I concur." Alice gave a strong nod and the short serpents hanging down over her forehead like bangs seemed to agree as they bobbed with the movement.

A memory—Clarissa springing the hug on him—brought a knowing smile to Ben's face. Gary had called his thinking of someone and then that person showing a 'third-eye.' As when he thought of Collins and out of nowhere, the jerk would appear, now, he'd just thought about Clarissa. Ben snapped his fingers and winked at Tex. "We're going to get her this time."

Tex stood on the dashboard. "How can you be sure? What if there are dozens of bags in there?"

"One of them will be her. I'm sure of it." As soon as the words left his mouth, a sense of dread—*hopefully alive*—stole over Ben and faded. He switched his attention to Alice as he got out. "We'll get you armed as soon as possible. If you get to your bagged sister before we get to my bag, get her out and back to the car." Ben extended a fist to Tex. "He and I can sneak the rest of the way."

Exuding confidence, Tex nodded solemnly and gave Ben a fist bump.

Alice rolled her eyes.

Tex leapt onto the paved concrete with a small *tink*.

Ben turned his companion loose. "Scout it out, buddy."

Tex saluted, hustled to the gates, slowed to peer both directions, then ran around the corner.

Closing the car door quietly behind him, Ben pulled the Anvilsmith to show the populating map on his screen to Alice. He glanced over his shoulder. Instead of getting out on her side and coming around, she walked across his seat and—*she doesn't have a belly button*—stepped over the driver door to stand next to him.

Almost dismissively, she said, "Uh, it reeks in here."

On the screen, Tex, represented by a green dot, moved along the white path to the red area of the building. As they moved to the entrance to the trash alcove, Ben thought about showing her the live feed through the pinhole camera between Tex's lenses. He struck the thought down. Last thing he wanted was for her to start thinking of his companion as a way to get a low angle up at... Well, up at whatever she might think.

Perhaps he'd gone to Meadows Towing too often, but parking his car next to a large machine meant for crushing made Ben look back to make sure the cardboard compactor hadn't reached out to snag his Transcend.

His car was gone.

"Where—" His heart flew into his throat. He felt the familiar sickening roll in his gut when he had come out of *Card Crafters* on his birthday to find that his car had been stolen. Preparing to properly yell and freak out, he swallowed to clear his throat.

Alice looked back at him. "What?"

In the brief moment it took him to find his voice, he spied the faint outline of his front fender, then his hood, the side panel, and the rest of the car. *It's virtually invisible in the shadows.* His head tilted. *Is it magic? The paint?* A faint chime came from his device.

Ben said, "Nothing." He looked back to the tablet. The green dot was still at the front of the building, but next to it, *+30*. Though excellent scouting work, Ben made a note to ask Tex later why he'd climbed to the roof.

"Two on the roof," Alice whispered. "Looks like it's time for me to get my weapons." She ran, leapt high onto the wall, and stuck. Stuck like gum, like glue, like Spider-Man. He'd seen her make contact, but hadn't heard even the lightest slap. Still, somehow, she stuck. Body close to the wall, she climbed to the top and slipped over a rain gutter to the rooftop.

Ben hustled to the corner.

External piping that ran up to dim lights affixed on the wall of every fourth building. Under the third one, where the orcs had deposited Alice, Tex descended from the roof.

Good thing he checked. I didn't even think about checking up there.

His companion dropped to the ground, lay on his

belly in front of the rolling door, and shimmied sideways into the building.

Ben checked his map to see Tex's relay of the inside of the building. The main area, fifty-feet wide had crates stacked forty-feet high at the far end, shortening the hundred-foot depth to eighty. Ben activated the camera feed and relegated the map to a corner of the screen. A catwalk ran along the right wall, above the crates, with an interior ladder just inside of the rolling door and another extending to the ground halfway through the warehouse. Three columns of boxes shone blue against the back wall. A legend popped up on the left of the tiny map in the corner, *blue = magic/magical*. Two more stacks lit on the screen, and then one of the Hawg motorcycles with high handlebars and equally high, long tailpipes.

What if Tex pops? Now would be the worst time for him to fry out and shut down. Ben whispered into the device, "Don't detect magic on items inside the warehouse. We're not going to capitalize on any of these, uh, *opportunities*."

Tex's words scrolled. "Are you sure? There is a magical motorcycle."

Though amused, Ben put on his game face. "Positive. Don't want to go all sunny-side up."

"Right." Tex flashed a frying egg on the screen. "Good thinking."

Ben laid a finger on his *Orion* spellcard and smiled at how easily he managed to channel Argosian energy into it. *Really nice to not have to fight Bastion to not use Nilosian magic to power my spells.* Like a property thrown boomerang, a nagging concern—*where's Bastion?*—pinged in his head.

Red flashes of light lit at Ben's sides. Two glowing gorillas, Abe and Oscar materialized. The light from them faded. Both had their weapons from a prior conjuring in hand. *Orion never did that.* Ben eyed Abe's greatsword and Oscar's daggers with an appreciative nod. Ben smiled at each of them. "I've got to outfit you guys better."

The gorillas hooted their agreement.

A chime. Ben glanced at his tablet. His eyes were drawn to a red dot on the map of the catwalk. Tex's text popped up. "One just came in—hot!"

Ben jumped onto Abe's back. "Go."

Chapter Thirty

GO TIME

ORION, the green gorilla Ben would conjure from inserting his spellcard into his tablet, never had a smell. He couldn't remember any of his conjurations having a scent.

Abe did. The coarse, red hair pricking Ben's hands and neck—expecting the teddy bear softness of Orion, Ben had almost let go—carried the bouquet of an exotic old growth forest. On Abe's crimson skin, the musky exertion of swinging tree to tree. In the pores, the grimy odor of a normal, completely wild life. Riding on Orion had been an exercise in luxury, perfect-suspension comfort when compared to this jostling Argosian creature. *I hope he doesn't have fleas. Please don't have fleas.*

Not burdened with extra weight, Oscar made it to the rolling door first. Pinning a knife in his red palm with his thumb, Oscar yanked the rolling metal door up with one arm. Before the door banged up, the gorilla had thrown his other knife into the warehouse.

A soft clatter followed the door smacking home in its sleeve. Oscar hurried in.

Ben let go of Abe as they turned into the warehouse. His loafers offered no traction and he slid a foot on the smooth concrete floor. *Two more seconds without line of site, Oscar, and you would've poofed away.*

Oscar grunted his understanding as he leapt up the crates toward where a limp body in blue jeans and a black biker coat lay on the catwalk. A short width of dark green skin—a couple of shades darker than hunter green, that Ben had started to call *warrior orc green*—showed between the coat collar and a full-face motorcycle helmet. In that small section of skin, the hilt of Oscar's knife. Not an inch of blade remained outside the orc.

Abe also vaulted up the crates to inspect the body.

Ben had forgotten how smooth the conjuror's bond between him and the gorillas felt both in combat and post combat. *It almost felt like we three are one.* As they could feel his thrill once he realized what they were doing, he could sense the intense focus on looting the body.

I don't have to get them better gear. Smiling a pleased smile, Ben shook his head against his earlier thought, and hustled to the ladder in the middle of the room. *They know what they want and where to get it.* Thinking about his fingerprints—*I need to get a pair of good gloves*—Ben hesitated for a moment. *Oh well.* He gripped onto a rung. The chill in the metal brought home the coolness of the night that the magic of his coat protected him again. *Yup gloves.* He started up and his loafer slid to the heel. *And better shoes. Maybe a set of the black boots—*

"Ben!" Alice yelled from behind him. Danger colored her voice. "Watch out!"

Five feet up, he turned to look at her.

At his new eye level, his gaze met a large set of bloodshot eyes, then flicked out to the massive brownish-green hand lashing out at him.

A tuzvul! Where the Hell—

It grabbed him by the ankle.

Ladder must've had a spell-trigger. Ben jammed his hand into his coat.

The strong hand closed hard around his ankle, squeezed with a vice-like grip, and yanked.

Pain shot through Ben's shoulder as the tuzvul yanked him free from the ladder. His hand missed his spellcards. His bone gave to the pressure. Agony—*it broke my ankle!*—raced up his leg and burst out through his lips in a jagged moan.

The tuzvul's other hand closed around his arm, the one going for his spellcards, and squeezed with remarkable strength.

He's going to break my arm, too.

It didn't break his arm.

The room spun as the monster hoisted him above its head.

Alice screamed, "Ben!"

Ben looked to Alice. The thin membrane over her eyes peeled back, revealing vibrant, glowing golden irises with tiny brown flecks. *Gorgeous.* A tightening, worse than any stomach cramp Ben had ever had, constricted his guts and rapidly spread outwards. His eyes went wide at the tightening in his chest and he could feel his consciousness weaken. *Check out time.*

Ben thought he'd be unconscious, but—*on reflex?*—he'd shifted his consciousness to Oscar and rode behind the gorilla's eyes as it left the dead orc on the catwalk and leapt over the railing.

From Oscar's point of view Ben saw his body, hoisted above the tuzvul's head, turn to gray stone. More than his body, his coat, his clothes, he could even glimpse the—now also stone—Anvilsmith tablet.

The tuzvul's lanky arms tensed and flexed.

Remembering how easily the dragon-tuzvul had torn a wing from his creature when the massive monster had gotten both hands on it, Ben cheered Alice's quick thinking. *I need to get out of here. I can only piggyback for an hour.* His thoughts went to his body. *I need to find Master Reynolds. He can turn me back.*

The tuzvul tensed once again, glanced up at the turned-to-stone body, and tossed it aside to swipe at Alice.

She ducked, jumped to the side, and rolled away.

The monster's other massive hand swooped.

She dodged again. The snakes down her back reared up, struck the tuzvul's wrist, and released as the arm arced over.

Oscar hit the floor. The Gorilla threw a knife. It sank into the tuzvul's chest where the heart would be. *Blades not long enough.*

The tuzvul's mouth opened and its throat worked as to bellow, but no sound came. It drove a fist down at Alice.

Alice planted a foot and rolled backward.

Abe soared from the catwalk and plunged his greatsword deep into the tuzvul's back.

The monster reared, its mouth open again to belt a muted roar.

It's silenced? That's why I didn't hear it. Ben took control of Oscar. He rushed forward to wrap the tuzvul's knee in a bear hug. *Time to return the favor.* He twisted. A pop from the monster's leg resonated through the ligament and vibrated against Oscar's chest. *Got you!*

The tuzvul's weight shifted to its other leg, and it swatted Oscar away with a massive backhand.

The blow cracked Oscar's ribs—*glad I can't feel that* —and sent him reeling. They scrambled for purchase as they slid through the warehouse and out into the alley, but found none. They slammed into a rolling metal door across the way.

Ben tried to rush Oscar back to his feet, mewing, the gorilla rose.

Inside, the tuzvul peeled Abe from its back and crashed the gorilla into the concrete. The smack opened Abe's hand and the greatsword clattered away.

Just about to transfer into his other conjuration still in combat, Ben hesitated when the tuzvul grabbed his gorilla with both hands, hoisted it into the air above its head, and wrenched to twist the shrieking gorilla apart.

"Hey!" Alice called to the tuzvul. It looked at her as the general glow around her eyes focused into golden beams which struck the tuzvul's eyes.

Flesh turning gray, the tuzvul kicked out at her with its bad leg.

Alice jumped back.

Turning more and more gray, the tuzvul returned its attention to ripping Abe apart. One last action before—

It became a statue.

Abe, painfully contorted in its frozen clutch, beat fruitlessly at the stone fist with his free hand. Only a jackhammer could get him free. Abe tried the stone fingers to no greater effect.

Come on, Oscar. Ben urged. *Time is against me.*

Cradling his cracked ribs, Oscar got back to his feet and beat out a hurried, lopsided shuffle to get back into the warehouse. Ben made him stop just inside the threshold.

Alice had gone to his turned-to-stone body.

What's she doing?

She leaned in close. Her serpents dangled onto his stone coat and around the stone head of his statue-self. She hovered her face close to his and—

No way.

Kissed him.

Chapter Thirty-One

FIRST KISS

STANDING in one of his conjuration's bodies, forty feet away from his own—which had been turned to gray stone—Ben gawked as he was kissed. Stunned, he didn't think about her being a medusa, he didn't think about having no real friends at his all-boys school to tell about this moment, and he momentarily forgot about the series of events that brought him here. The whole of his existence centered on feeling somewhat cheated.

Slowly, his sculpture-self turned back into flesh. Her serpents went back to form a bra as she warmed up a smile.

His body went limp in her arms. *It's reversible. Thanks goodness. That would've been hard to explain.*

Her soft smile faded quickly. "Ben?" Her eyes widened as she shook his body. "Ben?"

Ben went to answer, but wound up uttering a hoot. *Oh! I'm still in my conjuration…* Using Oscar's good arm, he smacked his forehead, then released control and landed back in his body.

Alice leaned in and kissed him again.

Though dry and thin, her lips possessed a gentle suppleness and malleability he hadn't expected. Between her having been in a bag and driving with the top down, he hadn't noticed her faint lilac scent. One of her hands cradled his head. The other lay on the side of his neck feeling for a pulse.

All right! With his lips, Ben pressed back.

She dropped him and wiped at her mouth as she reeled away sputtering. "You jerk!"

The back of his head smacked on the concrete. *Crap! My head! My leg!* Expecting blinding agony to shoot through him, Ben clamped his eyes shut and grimaced. *Ready.* But only a dull throbbing pulsed in his ankle. *Huh?* He opened his eyes and looked at his foot. *It's aligned with my leg and the pain isn't as intense as when the tuzvul broke it.* Gauging the pain, he equated it to a severe sprain. He extended his hand.

Oscar hooked his massive arm under Ben's armpit, grunted, and hoisted him up.

Standing on his good foot, Ben gingerly set his toe on the concrete.

From above them, Abe belted a helpless cry.

Ben glance up to his other conjuration and—*I've got you, buddy*—dispelled Abe. He did the same to Oscar, then touched the *Orion* spellcard and channeled Argosian energy into it to re-summon both gorillas.

As their red flashes lit next to him, Ben put more pressure and lifted his foot. *Now it just feels like I twisted it.*

Alice kept her distance. Sounding equally astonished, she muttered, "Impossible. I heard it snap."

"I *felt* it snap," Ben said, his eyebrows lifted and mouth wide in excitement. He didn't try to mask his amazement as he tried again and his leg supported his weight without any pain. Standing on it, he lifted his other foot.

"Humans don't regenerate." Alice's voice lowered. She took another step back. "What are you, Ben, really?"

She's right. Trying to find the source of the healing, Ben focused on the Komir necklace under his shirt. *Dormant.* His mind went for another possibility and came back empty. Though he had heard that only Hisboian casters could cast curative spells, he focused on his energy sources to see if magic flowed into his leg from either of them. *No, but…* His eyes shot wide. He grasped at his gut and stumbled.

"What?" Alice twitched as she started toward him, but decided to keep her distance.

Oscar and Abe both had their arms out to catch him if he fell.

Ben flailed his arms out and steadied himself. "I'm okay." He returned his hands to his abdomen. A warm, arcane resonance pulsed from the rumble within. *Is that another chakra opening?* He squeezed his stomach and power trickled as his gut gave a gurgle. *Yes! That is another power source, but it's not what's healing me.*

Alice asked, "Then what's wrong with you?"

Applying pressure to his stomach was like squeezing a sponge inside his gut. *Force equals magic.*

Alice said, "Ben."

Trying to focus on the amazing warmth within, he waved an annoyed hand at her.

She made a short disgusted noise and crossed her arms. "Really?"

Ben raised his arms.

Abe slid behind him and, as though about to give the Heimlich Maneuver, gripped Ben firmly. Slowly, Abe applied pressure.

Ben's stomach began to gurgle uncontrollably and series of oniony burps rolled up through him. He leaned his head back, teeth clenched against the tightening pain as the new magic source gushed more power into him. "I'm okay." He gazed into Alice's yellow eyes. *Her inner eye lids are down.* He tried to notice the brown flecks he saw in the amazing gold around the slitted pupil. Almost giddy, he blurted. "I have another font of arcane power."

Alice returned to mumbling. "...at what cost?"

Ben patted Abe over his shoulder.

The gorilla released him and retrieved his greatsword.

What does she mean, 'at what cost?'

Worse than her question, her face. The corners of her mouth dropped down and a concerned frown cast soft shadows over her eyes.

She's not talking about my magic... It's about the kiss. When Ben applied the context to her face—which probably couldn't have contorted any further into disgust—it sapped his joy at having a new energy source. "Oh, come on." Ben flipped his hands out and let them drop to slap against his sides. "It was an accidental kiss." *Not a hundred percent true, but she did kiss me first.* "If I'd thought about it, I would've told you that I can leave my body to piggyback, or control, my conjurations..." He trailed off. *Is it my breath?*

Alice had placed a hand over her nose and turned away.

Ben, you idiot. It's not about the magic or the kiss, or even your breath. It's about her sister. He walked toward Alice and—*in case it is my breath*—tried to empathize from a distance. "Is your sister's scent gone?"

She kept her back toward him and whispered, "I smell death..."

Oh shit. His Anvilsmith vibrated. Ben flipped his coat open to see the small map Tex had continued to update. A long hallway stretched out behind the door on the catwalk and seven red blips were rushing their way.

Oscar and Abe were already on their way across the warehouse floor.

Ben warned Alice. "Incoming!"

Chapter Thirty-Two

THE GAUNTLET

THE GORILLAS THUMPED up the crates, climbing to get into position on the catwalk. Ben considered casting his other three gorillas, but decided against it. *There's only so many that can fit at the door.*

Alice climbed the tuzvul statue and stood on its upturned face. She seemed focused on the door.

Ben couldn't ignore the feeling that she climbed up to escape being in his immediate presence. *She said she smelled death. I only smell the closed-in, recycled air.* Standing sideways, he used the tuzvul's leg as cover and slid his hand onto his spellcards.

The door flew open with a bang as an orc in jeans, a biker coat, and full helmet came through.

Oscar slit the first orc's wrists, making it drop its gun. Leaping over Oscar, Abe swung his greatsword in a mighty chop. The gorilla cleaved the first orc in two and dropped the one behind it with a deep gash down its front. Blood rained through the catwalk onto the crates.

The two gorillas jumped from the catwalk as the remaining orcs crushed in. They leveled their guns and shot at the retreating red apes.

Alice called, "Hey!"

An orc looked across the room at her.

Golden rays flashed from her to it

The orc turned to stone.

Ben pressed his index finger against his *Blast* card and maxed his flow into it. Three bursts of Argosian magic crackled as it rocketed from him to the line of orcs. The first two slammed into an orc, caving in its chest. The third blast passed through the one falling and smacked into the chest of the orc behind it with muffled cracks.

Oscar threw a knife.

The indented orc dodged. The blade took another half a spin. The hilt rang off the biker helmet of the one behind hit.

Another set of golden rays flashed from Alice before she jumped from the tuzvul, swinging around its neck to get behind it.

Three orcs—one graying to stone—had their guns trained on her.

Ben leapt in front of her.

The rapid crack of gunfire rang through the warehouse.

His Komir necklace pulsed a mad drumbeat against his chest as each bullet crushed against the magical force field it provided. The necklace quickly heated on his skin signaling that its limited battery would soon fail.

The bit of eyes Ben could see through the orcs faceplates became rounded. One spat a curse.

To keep the necklace from burning out—and burning him—Ben slid his pinky back to his *Shield* spellcard, dedicated one of his magic channels to it, and let his Argosian energy flow.

The necklace took the current of magic.

Ben shunted the rest of his max into his *Blast* spellcard. The two missiles slammed into an orc, knocking it from the catwalk onto the crates just beneath it.

His pendant cooled, drawing its power from his Argosian energy.

The last orc moved to retreat.

Oscar's other knife sunk into the back of the orc's knee.

The orc wailed in pain.

Abe tackled the biker from the catwalk, riding the creature to the ground. The orc crunched against the concrete floor.

Abe tumbled away.

Ben winced at the sound. He'd heard helmet and shoulder pad collide before—*the horrible wet snapping sounds*—he shuddered. *They were doing worse... Even when I try to justify it, it's still ending a life.*

A faint shuffling sound moved away from him. Ready for whatever, Ben turned.

It was Alice, as she put more distance between them.

What is your deal? You turn people to stone! The guilt he had started to feel for stealing a kiss had been put into quick perspective when weighted against killing. *She's changed so much. There must be something drastic that*

I'm missing. Use your words. Communicate. Ben steadied his voice and asked his question without hostility. "What is it, Alice? What's wrong?"

She looked ready to bolt. "It's just that—I've never known a caster who would do anything like what you've done."

The gloom over ending lives began to lift as her words struck a rarely strummed and unpretentious chord in him. *I wonder how many casters she knows.* His gaze dropped to his shoes and he shook his head against the reflexive mitigating thought. *Don't sully the compliment, Ben. She's saying you're special. Accept it.* Not knowing what to say, truly at a loss for words, a humble smiled spread his lips. Ben looked back to her face. *Her expression… The brow knotted, upper lip curled back, the corners of her mouth slightly downturned. That's not a look of amazement. She's horrified. Terrified. Why? Is being self-sacrificing a crime to her kind?*

His loss for words turned into a lack of concern. *I tried to understand. If medusas expect others to stand around and do nothing while they die, then let her be outraged.* He went to the ladder and, checking over his shoulder for another tuzvul, began to climb. His earlier thought flitted through. *Boots. Boots and gloves.* He marked both items on a mental 'to buy' checklist.

Every few rungs, he checked back. A tuzvul hadn't materialized to attack them and Alice remained rooted to the spot. "Time's ticking," he said. He glanced at his loafers as they made attention calling *clacks* on the catwalk. *These shoes aren't made for stealth.*

Abe hustled up the crates as Ben stepped over bodies, mentally apologizing to each for ending their lives as Oscar stripped them of the traditional daggers all orcs seemed to wear.

Ben kicked off his black dress shoes to stand in his school uniform dress socks, which were the same earthy brown as his school issued slacks. He shoved each shoe into the inner pockets of his coat, at the knees. *Better to have them tapping against me than waking up any sleeping guards.*

The Anvilsmith vibrated.

Ben checked it.

Tex had updated the map with a green arrow flashing down in the hallway beyond the door, the legend noting a possible magical trap. Tex had covered serious ground while they were still in the main warehouse. Again, Ben checked on Alice.

She'd backed out to the rolling door.

"Fine by me, Alice." He waved a dismissive hand at her. "If I find your sister, I'll free her and, if she'll ride with me, I'll drop her off at the Red Rocks."

Letting Abe lead, and avoiding the blood-wet parts of the catwalk, Ben followed Oscar through the door.

Chapter Thirty-Three

THE TRAP

THE WARM CORRIDOR began to darken. Ben's nose curled from the unfortunately familiar smell of orc body funk. *They should shower more often.* He had his gorillas pause. *Pretty soon it'll be too dark to see.* The brief hilarity he felt at the thought of orcs stumbling around and bumping into each other in the darkness got slapped serious. *You can't see in the dark, but they can!* Ben's eyes adjusted as much as humanly possible to the pitch black. Further in, barely distinguishable from the dark, he picked out areas with very dim glows.

The faint luminosity making him hopeful, Ben pulled his Anvilsmith, tapped *Spells*, *Enchantments*, *Elfsight*, and *Cast*. His Arcane Wattage counter ticked down by one to ninety-seven driving a point he'd missed—*I've mainly been using my own power*—as magic vibrated from his tablet into his fingers, making his eyes twitch. He grinned at the thought of being one step closer to being a true wizard. *Now, if only I could cast without anything in hand.* Where starlight would rain down outside, the hallway remained dark. Slowly, the few dim glows further down the hall seemed to intensify to offer pockets of light bright enough to see gray tiled floor between long sections of dark shadows.

Oh well. That'll have to be good enough. A light *thunk* sounded behind him. He spun.

A submachine gun in hand, Alice had pulled a clip from one of the fallen orcs closest to the door and its arm had flopped to the floor. Their eyes met for a brief moment.

Ben flinched and—remembering what she had said about the life of a medusa—fought the urge to look away. *That would be disrespectful.*

Alice, on the other hand, averted her eyes altogether as though he were the one in possession of a gaze attack.

She's making me feel like I'm the monster. Deep down he recognized that neither of them were monsters, but his offense at how her demeanor had changed made his thoughts superficial. He shook off wanting to yell—*just tell me what's wrong!*—at her. He shook it off again, presented the map on his tablet to her, and said, "The green arrow means a magical trap ahead. Do what I do."

She glanced at the map then angled her face away and mumbled something.

He stared at her, but she still wouldn't meet his gaze. *Don't let her attitude-change phase you Ben. Game face.* He had his gorillas start forward. *Game face.*

Abe and Oscar rushed down the hall and leapt through the area marked as a trap. Gauging it, Ben ran and leapt the same area. Nothing triggered. He had cleared the trap. Walking backward to give her room to jump, Ben waited to see if Alice would clear it, too.

A set of claws raked across his lower back.

He bellowed and dropped to his knees.

Alice raised her gun—

Oh shit!

She fired over him.

Rubble—*bullets*—rained on his back.

To get away from whatever had struck him, Ben tried to lunge forward to clear the trap. He got only a few inches away. It had hold of his coat.

Claws raked down his back, bumping down his rib cage like a mallet down a xylophone.

Incapable of expressing the pain, even in screams, yips, or cries, his mouth hung frozen open. He struggled against the coat for a moment before he twisted. His shoulders and arms slipped free. He flopped on the tile.

Ben rolled over to see his assailant. *Ahh!* His carved up back radiate pain. He arced up on his feet and shoulders from the agony of lying flat on his back.

More gunfire.

Grimacing, Ben rolled over on one shoulder toward Alice. He saw it. Them.

A stone demon, standing in front of a second stone demon, tossed his coat to the side.

Ben bellowed, "Gargoyles!"

"I know," Alice yelled back.

Claws outstretched, the closest one lunged at him.

Ben scrambled backward on the tile. He escaped the swipe only to hear a hollow *click* as he stumbled into the trap.

Powerful orbs pelted into him. Each broke open to blast a high-pitched sonic assault battering both his body and his ears.

He didn't know whether to shield his ears or try to guard against the brutal impacts.

A hand grabbed his collar and pulled him back.

Stone claws cut across his chest.

His abused ears alternated between piercing whines and deep ringing. The trapped area looked full of rippling bright blue water. He glanced back.

Alice had dropped the gun. Her mouth worked as she held her arm against her body.

"Back," he said, but couldn't hear his voice. He bumped her backward and fell on his butt. Pain rolled up his back flaring where he'd be sliced open.

The blue rippling kept the relentless statues at bay.

Beyond the trap, Ben could feel Oscar—*destroyed*—dissipate. "No!" He placed a finger on his *Blast* spellcard. Pointing at the first gargoyle, Ben channeled Argosian energy into his spellcard. Three bolts of energy flew from his hand, cracking it.

The gargoyle staggered, then recovered and lunged forward. Trying to fight through the bright blue air to get at Ben.

The trap beat the stone demon into gravely bits.

Ben sent another three blasts at the back of the other gargoyle.

It turned and charged at him, pulling up short just before the rippling air.

Abe slammed into the stone demon from behind and tackled it into the trap.

"Yes!" Ben pumped his fist. He quickly dispelled Abe before the trap beat him to bits.

The magical field battered the stone monster for a while before whatever powered the trap emptied and the rippling blue field winked out.

Badly cracked, the gargoyle pulled itself shakily to its feet.

Ben slapped his spellcard and finished the creature with three more blasts.

Breathing a sigh of relief, Ben stood. *So, the Komir necklace protects against magic and ranged weapons, but doesn't do crap for hand to hand.* The deep gashes on his back sang a choir of fresh pain as the movement had caused the closed wounds to reopen. *Duly noted.* He grunted and stood straight so they could close again. Curious, he pulled his shirt away from his chest to check the lighter slashes that streaked his chest. The cuts were closed with blood congealing over them.

Alice's words—*Humans don't regenerate*—came back to mind. He had been confused when she had asked, *What are you, Ben, really?*

Not being distracted by the joy of another magical font, Ben realized that her concern—coupled with Bastion having been in his head—was one hundred percent legit. *I wonder what the real answer to her question might be.* Ready to spring away, Ben inched onto the area where the trap had been.

The tiles *clicked*.

He leapt backward.

Nothing happened.

Still ready to leap, Ben rushed through the area to where his coat had been thrown. Carefully, he bent and picked it up. He examined the five vertical slashes across his lower back which formed an inverted "tee" with the horizontal gashes. He eased it on over his shoulders. *Neither of us would have gotten past this by ourselves.* Trying to get the words together to express his gratitude, he glanced back at Alice.

Cradling an arm to her stomach, she picked up the gun again. And, as though eye-contact with him contact would damage her soul, still refused to look at him.

Ben opened his mouth to say thanks, but clammed up. *Forget it. She's probably right.* The ringing in his ears eased. The pain from his back began to fade, and the cuts on his chest were now only scab and memory. He placed a finger on his *Orion* spellcard and channeled Argosian energy to summon Oscar and Abe. Of the two flashes of red energy, one materialized into Abe. But instead of Oscar, the second gorilla appeared empty handed.

It hooted at him.

Thinking hard for a moment, Ben recalled this gorilla from Meadows Towing last month as the one who had wrapped Toad up in chains. Unable to think of a human name for the conjuration on the fly, Ben smiled warmly and patted the gorilla once on its powerful chest. "Welcome back, Chainer." He pointed forward.

Abe led the way. Chainer followed. Ben fell in line.

He didn't turn his head to advise Alice. Her not looking at him would make him bring the topic to the table and—*she'd probably be closer to the truth I'd be comfortable with right now*—he sort of feared what she would say. "We're moving on."

The complex grew uncomfortably warm as they

moved down several long hallways, covering ground Tex had already mapped. Ben hoped to catch up to his companion.

Before they did, two brown dots appeared in a room with a red dot in each of the far corners. The legend updated, with a line stating brown indicated the presence of burlap bags.

Not attempting to look at Alice, Ben followed his gorillas and said, "We're getting close."

She didn't reply.

Ben held the device close to his mouth and whispered, "Good job, Tex. Go ahead and return to the car."

Tex's text window popped up. Entire sentences scrolled by faster than Ben could finish reading the first sentence. "Copy that, Ben. I'll be sure to send updates of the terrain on the way out and will send a warning if there's an ambush waiting at the car."

The small robot came around a corner at the end of the hallway.

Ben lowered his hand.

Tex raised his small metal hand, slapped him five, and kept with the plan.

Ben had his gorillas stop at the corner. He did, too. Glancing over his shoulder to catch a glimpse of Alice on his heels, he explained, "Okay. The gorillas go in first to draw fire. I go in next. If I call out 'caster,' you come in and try to get eye contact."

She didn't say anything.

In Adept Love's Dueling Hall, there was a saying painted on the back wall in foot-tall letters. *Through joint adversity, common bonds are formed. Let us grow hale and strong together.* Ben had only the one day in *Dueling* before his parents yanked him from the class. But he still remembered that saying and actually saw proof around the APA where the friendships built through the *Dueling* classes carried on while ones built in other disciplines faded at the end of the course. *This was my one chance to build a real battle-buddy* — the childish school term from three years ago felt ludicrous when applied in the real world—*and, somehow, I screwed it up.* Ben glanced back. "Could you at least nod that you understand the plan."

Still avoiding eye contact, Alice nodded.

He sighed. Without enthusiasm, Ben thought, *go time.*

Chapter Thirty-Four

TRUST, BUT VERIFY

With the increased heat in the deeper halls furthest from the warehouse entrance, the orc funk felt more pervasive. Almost like it could work into his skin to become Ben's own, constant stink.

Always smelling like an orc. The thought made him frown. He shook it off and considered the thirty-foot by thirty-foot layout of the room and the forty-foot hallway. *She should be okay.* He thought about the angles the two orcs could have on the hall if they simply moved to the middle instead of staying in the corners. *It would be horrible for her to make it this far to get gunned down here.* "Change of plans. Stay here around the corner."

He climbed onto Chainer's back and at first sniff decided he preferred to smell like the gorillas rather than the orcs. *Though neither would be preferable.* He sent Abe charging ahead to bash down the door. Chainer followed at the same breakneck speed.

Abe crashed through the door, knocking it from its

hinges. Automatic gunfire cracked the air. The gorilla stumbled a few feet into the room—*he's being shot from behind*—before being dispersed into crimson smoke.

Just short of the door, Ben let go of Chainer. Hand on his *Blast* card, he landed on his feet and slid.

The gorilla charged in, determined to take one of the orcs down before being dispatched, but only made it to the middle of the room before twitching away in red motes of fading energy.

Sliding just inside the door. Ben channeled the last of his Argosian energy into the spellcard. Four bolts flew from him, two sizzling toward each of his targets in the far corners. He turned to blast the orc to his right. *I'm out. His Argosian font had run empty. I didn't even feel it wane.*

The blasts hit the orcs in the corners. They dropped.

About to switch to cast with whatever magic swam in his belly chakra, Ben realized the one he pointed at had fainted. The other had his hands up with a dark spot—*not by design*—around his crotch and puddling on the floor.

Pointing at the still-conscious orc, Ben spoke in the Giant tongue that he had been learning from the orcs at Meadows Towing. With hard consonants meant to be barked with force, the language sounded broken and weak coming out of his mouth. "Down to the ground."

The orc dropped to his knees and then laid belly down in his urine.

Ben slid his finger back to *Orion* and thought about summoning gorillas with his new energy. *What if they're as uncontrollable as the one from the stable? This guy surrendered. The last thing I want is for one of my conjurations to beat him to death.* Ben cleared his throat and tried to lower his voice when he spoke Giant this time. "Stay still and live." *Did I say that right?*

The orc froze in place.

Guess so.

Gun at the ready, Alice charged in the room with her petrification membrane peeled back. Golden light bathed each orc as she looked and aimed at each. She focused on the one remaining still.

Bathed in gold, the orc remained face down.

"Please don't kill him or turn him to stone." Unable to stop either if she decided to do so anyway, Ben went to the orc who'd fainted. He kicked the gun away and pulled the dagger. "I told him he could live if he stays still and, since he's laying in his own urine, I'm quite sure he wants to live."

The light from her eyes dimmed as the inner eyelid dropped. Seemingly stunned, she dropped the gun and tentatively stepped to the first bag. She sniffed it. Moved past it, and sniffed the other. Alice hissed at the bag.

Hissing returned from within the bag.

Alice hissed a longer string, her forked tongue showing for a couple syllables.

Ben pulled his tablet and tapped *Translate* and *To Text* as they exchanged several rounds. The right box, the box meant to be translated into, flashed *English*. The left box, the box to be translated from, repeatedly flashed a small italicized sentences. *Waiting for input.*

Alice ran her hands along the woven-shut bag.

Good luck. Ben had found two people in similar bags

and neither had a way of opening them without cutting the bag.

Alice looked to him, her eyes not rising above his torso. "I need a knife."

Ben slid here the orc's blade hilt first.

She caught it and tried to cut at the top.

Ben went to the other bag and asked, "Hello?"

No response.

Alice asked, "Could you please help?"

"One moment." Being a jerk back to her didn't even occur to him as a viable option. Ben pulled his tablet, swiped back from *Elfsight*, tapped *Heracles*, and cast. His arcane wattage ticked down to ninety-six as the tablet pulsed magic into him. As though filled with water, Ben's muscles expanded in his shirt and pants. He put his hand out for the knife.

Still hissing with the other hisser in the bag, Alice handed it to him.

Ben pulled at a corner of the bag, drove the knife through, and ripped the top of the bag open. *That is some tough stuff. Even enhanced it's hard to rip.* For a moment, he wondered about Penelope's strength. She had been able to rip the bag she was in without much trouble. *It was probably a cheaper quality of burlap.*

Done with Alice's, he turned back to his.

Ben thought about the person in Alice's bag. *Her sister will probably be naked, too.* Ben slid his hand where the rips in his coat to feel for the slight vibration of the comfort knack. Nothing. *Ruined. Well, at least it could still cover her.* He transferred Malcolm's rusty nail and Clarissa's card to his pants pocket, pulled his shoes out, and handed his coat to Alice without eye contact. Ben said, "In case she wants something to wear."

About to hoist the other bag and carry it out, Ben cut into the corner to see strands of blonde hair and an orange coat. To be sure, he ripped the bag open and peered in. *Clarissa.* He beamed with pride. *I've done it! Now to get you back to the fairgrounds.*

Grateful that Clarissa was dressed, it occurred to him that he should've made sure before offering his coat for a woman who probably didn't mind being nude.

Alice's voice sounded a bit husky as she called from the door. "Thank you."

She doesn't seem like the emotional type; her voice is probably that way from not speaking. Ben looked to the door. Alice stood there. Beyond her—hissing up a storm —a second medusa, wearing his coat, ran out the way they came. Glad to at least have Alice back on speaking terms, Ben nodded to her. "You're welcome."

Alice made eye contact. The inner eyelids had been drawn back and the bright, golden serpentine eyes bathed him in light.

She's trying to turn me to stone! Ben averted his eyes. His hand went to his spellcard holder. He pulsed sizzling Nilosian toward his Orion card and waited for the tightening feeling of being petrified. While not what he wanted, he made his plan. *Cast the ape. Enter the ape. Beat her down.*

Nothing. He still felt normal.

The light extinguished. "Idiot-boy!"

Idiot-boy? Ben's teeth clenched behind his lips. When he glanced up to lock his gaze at waist height, she had already turned and left. *The snakes are longer than Alice's. Wait, was that the one we just saved who tried to turn me to stone? You filthy ingrate!*

Sizzling magic played at his fingertips. In the mass of snakes, he spied a red choker with orange trim. *Filthy, filthy ingrate!* With vibrating Nilosian energy around his hand, Ben barely managed to keep from casting gorillas to chase her. Instead, he opted for a threat. *No, a warning.* "You better hope we don't meet again!"

He didn't mean it. While he didn't expect a reward, a simple sincere 'thank you' would've been nice, but her attempting to turn him to stone made the words fly.

Ben slid his shoes on, hoisted Clarissa onto his shoulder and made his way back to the catwalk. He hustled down the crates and, huffing for the last two hundred feet, made it back to the car. Carefully, he lay the bag in the backseat.

At that moment everything, even Tex moving out from under the body, unfolded exactly like the vision he had seen in Papa Mojo's crystal ball.

A whining alarm kicked up in the night.

Ben leapt into the Transcend, put his key in the ignition, and—*why am I waiting for them when Alice's friend tried to turn me to stone*—waited for Alice and her sister to show. *Because, if they're on foot, they're screwed.*

A motorcycle roared past the opening, too fast for him to tell who rode it. Ben glanced to Tex. "Was that them?"

"Alice and another medusa?" His companion nodded. "Yes."

"Then we're out of here!" Ben pulled out of the trash

alcove and sped along the white line path presented on his Anvilsmith.

Out of the maze, he cranked the wheel to drift onto Dove Boulevard.

"Holy! What the heck is *that*?" He sucked in air and fully jammed on the brakes to stop. He gawked at what approached them from the opposite direction. "What is that?"

Chapter Thirty-Five

SO NOT STREET LEGAL

THOUGH BEN HAD NEVER UNDERSTOOD the purpose of most mundane vehicles, there had always been an implied logic to them. Alone, and need a cheap mode of transportation to get across town? Get a moped. Have more than one friend and the same goal? Get an econo-car. Want that ride in comfort? Get a luxury vehicle. Need to move big stuff across town? Get a truck. It all made sense, until now.

Five blocks ahead, a massive, matte grey vehicle—as tall as a semi-truck, wide enough to take up three of Dove's five lanes—rolled forward on some sort of treads instead of wheels.

With things like that rolling around, no wonder the streets are in such poor condition. As though also holding its breath against the rattling advance of the humongous car, the night had become still. The smog still hovered five stories up, placing a false, toxic, ceiling down the length of Dove Boulevard until the brown sky met with the blacktop sandwiched vertically between industrial sprawl.

Tex's own shock or disbelief at what he saw made his synthesized voice came out flat. "That's a tank, Ben."

A tank? Coming his way, the treads slowed as though the massive thing wanted to change directions, but physics demanded it follow the same rules as any other vehicle without specific enchantments to tell nature that the rules don't apply right now. *I wonder what's it for. It's huge! You probably could fit a dozen people inside.* Though it didn't look like a comfortable ride, Ben tried to equate it to things he knew. *Perhaps it's what mundanes use when they have particularly heavy stuff to move.*

The tank came to a stop. The loud, unmistakable gurgling pipes of a distant Hawg motorcycle momentarily stole Ben's attention.

Down Dove, shifting lanes, the motorcycle carrying Alice—*and her ungrateful sister*—zoomed away.

"Ben," Tex's voice had taken on a sense of gravity. "That's a tank."

Ben replied, "I heard you the first time, buddy." Still marveling, he thought, *I wonder what it's for?*

A faint, almost dainty, *thunk*, like striking an air conditioning vent with a small hammer, sounded. Somehow the sound made the massive tank rock back and a gleaming white chunk of light—*too slow to be real light*—sped away from the tank. That nearly oblong hurtling object arched gracefully before beginning to descend...

Right. At. The motorcycle. Ben's eyes went round with

realization. He tried to will them to see what he saw; to know what he knew. He projected his thoughts, *Watch out!*

Before the light got to them, the Hawg motorcycle, and the riders on it, disappeared. No evasive maneuvers taken, they were—*How? Where?*—just gone.

The white blast landed just to the left of where the motorcycle had been heading. A pure, snowy hemisphere of light, taller than the surrounding buildings, filled all ten lanes and expanded into the neighboring alleys. Dirt kicked up from the street around the white dome as a shockwave blasted around it.

Tex had raised its volume with dire intonations. "Ben, that's a *tank*!"

The distant rolling force came.

Estimating he'd be unable to get all the way back into the alley in time, Ben backed the Transcend up so the tank lay between them and the coming wave.

As though the tank was nothing more than an open window on a gusty day, the rolling wind disturbing the dust and debris on Dove washed over and through Ben, Tex, and the car.

A tiny percentage of his remaining energy snuck away—ebbed if you will—by the wind which had pushed through them and continued to roll. *Why does my Argosian chakra itch?*

Bastion, the four-armed gorilla Ben had hoped was gone, glanced around in his Nilosian font for a moment before rolling over to utter a slightly annoyed, but mostly contented, grunt.

His—*ours?*—Nilosian energy sucked the beast down

into the chakra. *It's still in me?* A sudden hopelessness stole over him. *How do I get rid of it?*

"Go, go, go." Tex's volume maxed out. "Go!"

Ben stomped on the accelerator. The Transcend shot into the alley across Dove. "What the heck *is* that?"

Tex answered, "It's a *tank*!"

"Yeah, Tex. I got that!" Ben made a left to run parallel with Dove. "What's it for?

"Killing, you fool."

Fool?

Machinegun fire cracked into the night. Echoed through the desolate alleys.

Tex spun in his harness. "Good call on the turn."

Ben glanced back through his rearview mirror. White energy streaks became smaller as they flew across the corridor

Tex faced the console. "We'd be Swiss cheese if you had kept going straight."

Ben acknowledged, "Thanks. Find us a path back to the freeway."

"Will do."

As though they were driving on any two-lane street, the alley provided clear going. *Can't imagine what this would be like without the alcoves for trash.* Ben's gaze went to the rearview mirror to where the Anvilsmith Dome loomed, completely blotting out the horizon. Ben slowed.

"What is it?" Tex asked, "What's wrong?"

Something's not right. Ben stopped and turned back to focus on the buildings the light shot through and voiced the oddity, "There's no damage from the bullets.

Bricks should be being torn away, and glass should be shattering."

The robot turned again and whirling—Tex's ocular sockets twisting—sounded. "Those are *magical* bullets, Ben."

Ben faced forward. He jammed the accelerator. "Get us out of here, and away from the tank."

His companion touched the screen and a path of five turns, starting with a short run and two diagonals, showed the way back to Main Street and the on-ramp.

Ben broke, turned, and floored it again.

The Transcend revved hard from the surge, accelerated to sixty miles per hour before something clunked under his hood and his car started losing power. "Oh, crap!" He glanced to Tex. His gazed jumped to check the Anvilsmith. They neared the turn. "We must've been hit."

"No." Tex tapped the tablet and a '55' popped up at the intersection.

Ben whipped around the corner at precisely fifty-five miles an hour, and then they were on a long straightaway.

Tex continued, "I set a program to not exceed the max turning speeds and—"

A buzzing in the sky caught their attention. Above them, a metallic hummingbird kept pace with the car as Ben accelerated to eighty miles per hour.

As though it had to be voiced, Tex said, "Not good."

Holding the wheel steady with a hand and a knee, Ben ran a finger along the card holder to his bald eagle spellcard. With more reason now to not trust the Nilosian energy than ever before, he channeled from his

new font. Deep violet energy—*Krotosian magic!*—
flashed his bald eagle into existence.

The purple conjuration appeared and snatched at
the metal tracker with its talons. *Tinks* sounded it
scoring twice, but the tiny machination moved too fast
for the conjuration to keep hold.

Flying as quickly as it could to keep up, his eagle
continued to lose ground.

Trailing them, streaks of white light came from
about where the tank had been on Dove Boulevard.

The bird's a tracker! Gotta drop it. Unable to point at it
without significantly increasing the chance of wrecking,
Ben recalled Tex's ability to transfer energy between
Anvilsmiths and yelled, "Point at it!"

Tex swiveled in his harness and pointed.

"Become a conduit." To keep his speed, Ben hit
cruise control and braced his knees against the steering
wheel. He touched his *Blast* spellcard and—*hope he don't
pop*—channeled the Krotosian spell through his
companion.

A violet blast flew from the small robot's hand.

Tex swung its fist through the air. "Count it!"

In Ben's mirror, the mechanical hummingbird
dropped to the blacktop behind them and skidded like
a shuttlecock.

The white streaks still closed on them.

Ben jammed on the brakes, took a left on a street
that put them on a diagonal back to Dove.

The white streaks behind them stopped.

Ben slowed and made another turn that looked like
it would do the trick. To be sure, he said, "Reroute us to

the freeway again, Tex, and keep an eye out for those flipping birds."

Tex tapped the Anvilsmith again. Shades of gray showed the various ways back. All of them took them a long way around either west or north to avoid a large, walled industrial complex. "Nothing for it, Ben." His companion shook his tiny head. "We need to double back."

"No." Ben ran his finger up the screen. The least dingy gray line, indicating the best route, kept dancing around buildings trying to correct for him not following any of the alternate routes suggested as his finger ran up the street. With each adjustment by the map, the device flashed 'Turn around.' The line they were on darkened to being the worst route as he pushed his fingertip closer to the wall. If not for outlining one-half of an expansive corporate lot, the line would've been straight. *And, once on the other side, we'd be only one slanted street away from getting onto the freeway.* Ben asked, "Do you know what I want you to do?"

"The thing you've been wanting to do since you read about it in the owner's manual," Tex replied, punching a code—*one, eight, one, one, three. Got it!*—into the console. "It's meant for mundane walls, Ben. If this wall has any sort of magical reinforcement…" Tex didn't finish. He let the rest hang in the air.

He's right. Ben sighed. He wanted to ram through the wall. *This is the wrong time to needlessly toy around. Better double back and*—

A humming closed in on them.

Tex called out, "Bird!"

Heading directly at the barrier, the car began to

slow. Ben ordered, "Remove the limiter." Tex complied before he finished the sentence. The engine revved to life and they rocketed toward the wall. Speedometer rolling past a hundred, The Transcend moved faster than the hummingbird could fly.

It dropped down to drift behind them, which—somehow—allowed it to keep pace.

"Aim at the bird." Ben didn't dare to let go of the wheel. Not yet.

"It's gone," Tex said. "Up and away."

Like a space shuttle reentering the atmosphere, the front of the Transcend had developed a faint green force filed.

The towering, tan, cinder-block wall drew closer.

The force filed grew darker.

Ben's knuckles when white on the wheel.

Closer.

He clenched his teeth.

Closest.

His body tightened. *Bye Tex.*

Crash!

Chapter Thirty-Six

BACK TO THE BIG TOP

THOOM!

Boom!

The world went dark as they rammed through brick, sand bags, and another layer of brick. *The world's shortest tunnel.* Shattered chunks and debris flew far and wide. They pulled sand in their wake which trailed away from the punched-open wall like a comet's tail. The mess danced behind the Transcend and settled in the empty parking lot.

They were back in the open air. The smoggy ceiling still hung over them and denied the moon's proper glow to shine through. The wide, dark building in the center of the lot didn't have any lights on. Keeping an eye out for any change, Ben passed it. *No parking lanes, no curbs, no front gates...* "Tex, what is this building?"

His companion tapped on the Anvilsmith.

They shot through the lot and exited through the parking lot's proper front entrance.

Tex answered, "Don't know. It's not listed."

On the final straightaway, Ben eased his foot a little further down and the speedometer steadily rotated to the right with their increasing speed. A glint of steel —*the bird*—showed in the rearview. It grew smaller...

And smaller...

Gone.

Ben slowed for the onramp, then sped back up to eighty miles per hour. "Tex, mind the traffic behind us—"

"To see if we're being followed." Tex cut in. "On it."

Cutting through the thin traffic, Ben's gaze occasionally bopped from the freeway ahead and to his mirrors to check the traffic behind them.

Tex advised, "No one is following us."

We're supposed to be followed... Ben shook his head as he slowed to fifty-five. Ben glanced at Tex and hoped. "Are you sure?"

His companion touched the Anvilsmith where they had gotten on the beltway from Old Henderson. "No headlights pulled on after us." The robot ran his hand up the freeway. "We have been doing nothing but overtaking cars, none of which have been acting erratically as if to keep up with us." He added, "From what I've seen, every car we passed reacted to our speed, then returned to normal driving." Tex clapped his small metal hands with a *tink* to indicate *case closed.* "Either we're in the clear and the Mystique is making the mundanes act as though nothing happened—or we're just in the clear."

Where's the pursuit? Clarissa's in the bag... Unless—I should've swept the whole complex for bags—unless, maybe, she has a sister, too, and that's who I have. Ben slapped his leg and steered toward the exit for Eastern. "Damn it, we should've swept the entire complex."

Ben hadn't used magic since getting on the freeway. There hadn't been a need. Every Adept at the APA harped on how using too much around mundanes would 'break the Mystique,' which would be bad for all mystics. He had heard about the Mystique all his school life, but no one ever explained what *It* was. He had gotten a look at It—at least he thought he had—in the psychedelic aura around Alice. *If the Mystique keeps mundanes from registering arcane effects, can it be strengthened? How much can the Mystique cover?*

He went down the off-ramp and stopped at a light.

Ben drew a breath, relaxed his mind, and let the air out. They'd slowly circle back. *Hopefully the alarm would be called off by then.*

Starting to feel a little hungry, he scanned the mundane fast-food places his mother loathed: Jill in the Cube, *line's too long,* Caliente Chicken, *closed,* and Pizza Kings. *Sure could go for a slice.*

Not certain if his stomach could handle the grease, Ben picked up the antacids, popped a cherry disc in his mouth, and checked the rearview mirror again. *Nothing.* He eyed the two cars that had been waiting for a left turn to Eastern. *Neither are of mystic make.* "I know you're always sure, Tex. Sorry for asking."

The robot leaned back in his harness. "Forgiven." His small shoulders lifted and fell as though heaving a sigh, too. "After what we just went through, double—even triple—checking is entirely understandable." He motioned to the back seat and flipped his puncturing sliver. "Are we going to pull over and let her out?"

The light turned green. Ben eased on the accelerator. "I guess." He pressed his lips together. *We're supposed to be followed...* "I really don't want to say this, buddy, but we might actually have to go back to Old Hendo again."

"What!" Tex sat up in his harness. "Why?"

He took in a deep breath to explain. "Well—"

A rapid howl closed on him. Pain rocked his shoulder forward as the world flashed purple.

Krotosian magic. The blast broke his budding melancholy. *On the city streets?* "Find the source." Ben gave the Mystique half a thought, *worse comes to worse, I'll breach.* He stomped on the accelerator.

A purple bolt of magic cast its light over him and his car as it missed.

Behind us and to the right. He began to swerve to make for a harder target.

"There!" Tex called. Two blips pinged into position on the Anvilsmith beyond the Eastern off-ramp.

Ben glanced over his shoulder. In the dark, under the freeway overpass, two Stingers—*the same ones from before*—lit up light green and purple.

They started after him.

A part of him admired their casting ability. *Wow, that's some distance to hurl a blast.*

The headlights of both cars dimmed to a deep violet for a moment. Krotosian magic bolts flew from their fenders toward him.

Whoa! That explains the distance. Ben cut across two lanes to dodge. "Their cars have weapons!"

"Illegal," Tex *tsked* inflecting sarcasm into his voice. "Where's a Magistrate when you need one?"

Speeding, Ben started to catch up to a small patch of traffic. "I know where." He planned his maneuvers.

A horn blared as he hooked around and nearly sideswiped a mundane car as he passed it.

His pursuers didn't fire.

They care about the Mystique. Good

Five long streetlights from the Samhain Festival, Ben sped away from the mundanes as the Stingers began to close some of the distance. *If I blast out a tire from each mundane car, there will be a pile up and the Stingers won't be able to get through.* While a solid strategy and, possibly, the correct tactic, Ben didn't act on the passing thought. *There are still alternatives.*

Where Ben had cut rudely through traffic, the Stingers seemed to purposefully make bad moves to allow the mundane traffic to block them.

Are they even trying to catch me? A crazy thought—*I should stop*—flew through his head when he spied the first entrance to the Samhain starwise parking.

All the lights on both Stingers flashed and they rocketed down Eastern.

Whoa! Ben cranked the wheel and jammed on the brakes to power slide into a drift. He jumped back on the accelerator and his Transcend banged sideways into Red Lot Five's wrought iron entrance fence. With his foot still down, the tires spun and shot him forward.

The Stingers' speed-boosting spell, unlike his, didn't end when, as though on rails—*just like the Legerity*—they peeled into the lot a few precious seconds later.

Ben shook his head as the lit cars grew closer in his mirror. "I don't like this, Tex."

"Neither do I," Tex started to punch a code into the console.

A muffle arose from the burlap bag.

Ben yelled over his shoulder, "You're almost safe Clarissa!" He made one more turn which put him in line with the entrance to the fairgrounds proper. Lowering his voice, he spoke to Tex. "No, I mean, there's magic going on in the parking lot." He spared a glance at his companion. "Papa Mojo said the Primaries would show."

"Did he?" the robot asked, then proposed, "Maybe Mojo lied?"

Racing down the row of cars, Ben shook his head in disagreement and opened his mouth to say so, but he couldn't think of an alternate possibility. *The diviner duped me into being a delivery boy.* A desperate desire to punch Mojo's floating face, rose, then faded. *This is not the time for frivolous anger. Focus. Get her safe.* He pointed to the Anvilsmith. "Give me turn velocities again, Tex."

With one tap, the turns into each lane came up with numbers indicating the speed he should not exceed.

The lights on the Stingers dimmed and their amazing speed faded.

They can corner, but their speed spell doesn't last nearly as long as mine. While good to know, they had closed enough distance that he couldn't stop and let Clarissa out at the concrete pillars between the wrought iron lions.

Another string of muffles came from the bag.

"Tex." Ben pointed at the pillars. "Are those columns magically reinforced?"

Tex popped above the dashboard. Its optics whirred. "Yes."

"Knew it." Ben eyed the speed on the final turn. *Forty-five and I'm going sixty.* Not ready to hit his brakes as they sped down the rows of cars, Ben touched his *Orion* spellcard and channeled energy from his gut. Violet magic flashed and howled as his immature reserve emptied. A purple gorilla appeared in the backseat. The suspension creaked at the sudden increase in weight.

Unlike the insta-bond he felt when he cast Abe and Oscar, or the automatic bond when he would cast plain old Orion, Ben had to establish the link between him and Krotosian-based gorilla.

Mentally giving his order—*lift the bag and protect it, when I turn, as you leap onto the fairground*—Ben slammed on the breaks. Leaving a line of smoke behind them, the Transcend's tires belted out a whine as they skidded across the blacktop.

As directed, the gorilla lifted the burlap wrapped Clarissa and leapt hard—*too early!*—when Ben cranked the wheel to hit the turn—skidding—at forty-four miles per hour.

Cradling the bag, the gorilla landed and rolled onto the fairgrounds. *Go further in.* Ben glanced at the gorilla through his side mirror and ordered. *Further. Further.*

The gorilla jogged further, and further, and stopped.

Keep going in until you dispel. That should do the trick. Though he meant to check on his gorilla, Ben's gaze locked on Malcolm coming out from between cars. The bully pulled up his pants as the two lit Stingers made the turn behind him. *Pooping in the parking lot, Malcolm?* A quick laugh burst from Ben's mouth. *Really?*

Ben eyed the last bend that would put him en route to the exit onto Sunset Drive. *Everyone who's starwise is here, but there's no way I can make it onto the fairground without either wrecking my car or having them catch me.*

Tex tapped the Anvilsmith. The map zoomed out to a wider, top-down view of the area. "Where to now?"

Ben tried to think of a safe place—the safest place—to go, and came up empty. Almost in protest to what he considered next, his gut gurgled. *Two birds with one stone? If not, perhaps one bird will kill the other...* He took another antacid, narrowed his eyes and said, "Chart the best path to Meadows Towing."

Chapter Thirty-Seven

NO SAFE PLACE

THOUGH BEN WOULD'VE PREFERRED GOING BACK down Eastern to the freeway, the Stingers had hit their speed boost spell as they pulled onto Sunset Road behind him. In reaction, he had Tex use their last one. They rocketed up the backside of McCarran Airport. While the Stingers' enchantment gave them better control, the Transcend's boost going well past Grier Drive. As though he were trying to drag-race the roaring plane taking off on the jetway on the other side of the chain-link fence.

The speed doubled, if not tripled, the night's chill and he longed for his slashed-up school coat. Even with the comfort enchantment destroyed, the physical coat would've offered some protection.

As Ben's nose filled with the pervasive plane fumes, he grinned at the thought of his pursuers' nostrils filling with his proverbial dust...

However, they continued to chase. Onto The Strip, past Town Square, onto the 215, and out toward

Pahrump. *They're waiting for me to make a mistake.* The Stingers kept on giving chase. *Why are they fixed on me?*

Ben took the off-ramp where the freeway curved away from civilization and turned at the bottom to the long, straight-shot to Meadows Towing. Not slowing, Ben checked his mirrors in snatches. The two glowing imports came down the exit, then made two quick turns to take the on-ramp heading back to the city.

Finally! Ben applied his brakes to slow and stop.

Even at a distance, he could spot their neon lights driving away. "Well." He took a deep breath of the clean desert air, and exhaled, "I guess that's that."

"Stingers away," Tex remained focused on the Anvilsmith on the center arm rest. "Only one more."

Ben tilted his head. "One more?"

"Yes." Undoing his harness straps, Tex motioned to the tablet with his head. "Take a look."

Ben picked up his Anvilsmith. *The Legerity?* Two red blips, the Stingers, moved away while a yellow blip closed in.

Tex continued. "In tracking the two Krotosian cars, I noticed a distant set of headlights speeding through traffic to catch up."

Ben scanned the dark land around the long road he had stopped on. The bright purple neon star sign above Meadows Towing shone alone, like a clasp holding the night's smothering cloak closed over the surrounding desert. Back the way he came, the freeway streetlights and car headlights came just so far from civilization before arcing back away from what the orcs called the Might-Lands.

He quick tapped through the menus to switch from

Heracles to *Elfsight* and cast it. The Anvilsmith vibrated in his hand as the awatt meter ticked down to ninety-five. The stars' light began to rain through the darkness as the magic settled into his eyes. Still taken with the effect, Ben sighed at the beauty. *Doubtlessly, first place would've been mine if I entered this as my Spell Programming project in the Magic Fair, but then everyone would make knock-offs of it... And that would cheapen this.* He put his hand out. Light pooled briefly in his palm, evaporating nearly as quickly as it formed.

A pair of headlights came down the exit. Since a majority of students in the Las Vegas Valley drove the exact same model as his, Ben knew the shape of headlights well.

A Transcend... Ben holstered his Anvilsmith and got out of the car. *I'd bet both my tablets that it's Malcolm.*

Tex asked, "What are you doing, Junior Apprentice?"

"I think I know who this is." Ben answered, then realized what Tex had called him. Prior to the Node Key popping the robot's settings, his companion had always identified him by his title since that was how he'd introduced himself to his, then, new companion. He glanced at Tex who appeared to busy himself with work on the car console when none was needed. "Why'd you call me Junior Apprentice?"

Tex lowered his head, processed the question and did not look up when he answered, "This is not a wise course of action. As such, it triggered a permission subroutine. While your title slipped out, I was able to stop the subroutine before it made me ask you to contact an Adept to advise you." Tex's optics moved to look into Ben's eyes, the metal plates on the robot's brow layered to imitate a furrow. "I was hoping you hadn't noticed. Hope I didn't offend you."

"Meh." Ben waved a hand to dismiss the issue. With *Elfsight* active, the set of headlights coming from the freeway shone like a pair of searchlights moving in tandem. He shielded his eyes and made out the physical shape of the Transcend. *And there's those silly buffalo horn-nobs Malcolm had added.* "Mind the off-ramp, Tex. Let me know if any other cars start coming our way."

Tex climbed to the dashboard. "What are you doing now, Jun—" The robot cut his sentence. "Ben?"

This must seem like a really bad idea if it triggered another subroutine. Ben started to fold back the right sleeve of his dress shirt. A small part of him—the part that didn't want to possibly taint the school's name with his decision to duel outside of the night's Shenanigans—thought to remove his red school tie. *Even though it'll just be me and him.* Ben whipped his tie off and tossed it in the backseat. He answered, "Waiting for Malcolm."

Tex's optics whirled fast and its voice took on a faint echo. "Confirmed, the car has the same profile, after market add-ons, and color scheme."

Folding his left sleeve back, the odd sound made Ben eye his companion. The robot's optics completed quick turns, so at least it didn't look like he was going to shut down again. *Not hardware, then. Something must be going on with his programming.*

Ben asked, "Still with me, buddy?"

Tex took no notice of the question. "Confirmed. The license plate is the same as before."

Ben leaned in to look at Tex's optics from the side to make sure they weren't silently going haywire. The small binocular sockets inside the lenses made quick, controlled turns.

"Confirmed. The driver's face fits sonar concave mapping belonging to Malcolm."

"Tex?" Ben reached out his for the robot and stopped short to bite his lip. *I really hope he doesn't kick off a shock.*

The robot's optics shifted slightly to the left twice. "Concave mapping does not recognize the passengers."

"Passengers?" Ben turned.

The car zoomed closer.

He shielded his eyes as *Elfsight* lit three auras —*casters*—inside the car. Ben focused on them to discern what type of magic they used.

The high beams flicked.

"Ah!" He covered his eyes and leapt into his backseat.

A rush of air sucked at his slacks and his car rocked as Malcolm zoomed past. *That was close!*

"Verified." Tex continued, "Passengers are unknown."

Tires squealed.

Ben sat up and tried to rub the bright spots in his vision away.

Tire smoke rose up and away as people got out from both sides of the car. A Krotosian—*Malcolm*—got out from the left. Two Nilosians—*who are they?*—dashed from the right and out into the desert.

Malcolm yelled, "I've come to get my hook back!"

Ben hopped from the backseat onto the street. "Tex, stay vigilant of the unknowns and advise if they close in."

"Confirmed. Orders received."

Ben scanned. His spell helped him spot the Nilosians, who ran a good distance away, stopped, and turned to watch, seemingly. His pinky found his *Usain* spellcard. *I'll go head's up against Malcolm any day, but if they join in…* Ben struggled with his ego, which tried to convince him that he could take all three. He kept his pinky in position. *Just in case I have to split.*

Stepping away from his car, Ben focused on Malcolm.

The Dunn-Blatt moved purposefully to be at fifty-feet away for a mid-range duel, stopped, and pointed. "Give me back my nail, Ben, and I won't break you."

The onion taste started to rise in Ben's throat as the font in his gut swelled, oozing a small amount of Krotosian energy. He swallowed. "In consideration of the great many A. P. A. students you hooked before they were ready, I'm going to say no."

Elfsight showed purple power pulse from Malcolm's center. It shot up to his shoulder in the same manner Ur-Krurk's energy had when the ogre had hurled a magic blast at him.

If I have the wrong spell—don't think about it. Ben channeled the thrumming green energy from the Anvilsmith, through him, and to his *Blast* card to negate the Dunn-Blatt's spell with his own.

The magic moving within Malcolm faded as his mouth dropped open in astonishment.

Oh, what I wouldn't give to have a picture of that face! Talk about priceless.

"So, you can counter-spell?" Malcolm recouped and gave Ben a small nod. "Not bad, Baby Ben. Not bad at all. And here I thought this would be a brutal, one-sided fight that would only end with you licking my shoes, but I want that ability—so now, I will have to kill you, *if* you don't return what is mine so I can steal what's yours."

What the hell is he babbling about? Ben stole a glace to the Nilosians. *There's still at a distance, but what do they want?* He turned his attention back to Malcolm.

Malcolm began to dance in place as if he were Bruce Lee and his deep violet Dunn-Blatt school-issued jump suit leant an eerie validation. "This is your last chance to give up my hook or shit gets real."

Ben opened his mouth to reply…

Chapter Thirty-Eight

ON A DARK ROAD

...AND PAUSED. He dug his hand into his pocket and rubbed the coarse, rust-covered nail that Malcolm truly seemed ready to kill for. *I've wanted to duel him for years, but in a civilized way. With my Argosian font drained and my Krotosian chakra too immature, I'd have to resort to Nilosian if my tablet runs out. and may stir*—he didn't want to even think Bastion's name for fear of waking it —*The Beast.* Ben stole another glance to the two Nilosians standing off in the distance, watching. Somehow, they—*Collins and Papa Mojo?*—factored into this.

Malcolm has more dueling experience... The night's chill started to seep into his bones. Ben shivered and fended off a sneeze. *Am I willing to die in the cold, on a dark desert road over*—he rubbed the nail again—*something so trivial as a tether?*

"Ben." Malcolm called. "I can serve up this whoopin' however you want it." The Dunn-Blatt stroked his nose twice with his thumb before going back to his Bruce Lee stance. "Do you want this over hard, or over easy?"

Ben narrowed his eyes at Malcolm. Between thinking it over and Malcolm's boasting, he found his reason to lay it all on the line tonight. *It's the principle. If I let him bully me, yet again, when will I ever take a stand?* He thought about the duel he'd had with Jack who must've had dozens of duels under his belt. Though he had not beaten Ur-Krurk through dueling, the ogre's tactic would be the difference. He released the nail to let it fall in his pocket.

Instead of answering, Ben executed the courtly fifteen degree bow duelist were supposed to exchange.

A bow that Malcolm didn't return.

Sneering The Dunn-Blatt's body shuddered and shook as he dragged both of his hands across his abdomen and raised them high into the air. The energy at Malcolm's center undulated and rolled. He yelled, "This ends now!" A shot of Krotosian flew to Malcolm's shoulder while a second zoomed toward his throat.

Ben slapped his spellcard holder, channeled power into his *Blast*—the magic at Malcolm's shoulder poofed away—and *Orion* cards. The summoning spell sped up Ben's spine toward his throat. Instead of calling a green gorilla, Ben gambled and turned the magic to counter Malcolm's other spell.

The cone of violet light exiting Malcolm's mouth started to form his conjuration before winking away. "You can dual-cast, too?" Malcolm ground his teeth. "Duly noted." His face twisted into an offended scowl. "You can only counter with the exact same spell. So, which Dunn-Blatt taught you how to throw a dusk buffalo?"

Ben shook his head. "I don't owe you anything. Especially not answers."

"Fine! I'll beat it from you!" The purple in Malcolm's gut blossomed before diminishing by half as two glowering orbs began traveling up his torso.

What spell is that? Ben slid his fingers on his spellcard holder to channel energy into *Usain*, *Leap*, and *Shield*. The tablet vibrated. His legs became inhuman springs as the orange tang of Usain filled his mouth. Used to hooking his Shield spell into the burnt-out Komir necklace, he'd forgotten about the minty smell of the air hardening around him from *Shield*.

Gotta change that.

Malcolm pointed at him.

Keeping the Dunn-Blatt in his field of vision, Ben ran away from his car out into the desert

The pulsing tennis-ball-sized spheres, hallmarks of the most well-known evocation spell, whistled into being.

Cody would cream his pants.

The howling from the Krotosian magic's increased as the orbs flew closer and exploded into massive fireballs.

Ben leapt hard.

He out-legged the first's blast radius, but not the second. The fire burned against his shield as he flew through the air. The protective force began to crack. Heat poured through while blazes licked around the barrier. The protection faltered. The mint scent ceased. Shoes smoking, Ben landed and rolled just outside the second ball's radius. He ground his loafers into the dirt to smother the flames and disperse the heat.

A sense—*I'm going too far*—tugged at his spatial awareness. *Must be near ten times the starting dueling distance. Any further and I forfeit.* He stepped backward which violated the tenants of the Usain spell. The orange taste and spell benefits vanished.

Malcolm's remaining energy drained away as two more glowering purple orbs traveled up to his shoulders.

Glowing spheres appeared in Malcolm's outstretched hands.

If only I knew Fireball. I'd love to counter those.

The Dunn-Blatt waved his hands in small circles. "Last chance, Baby Ben!"

Darting back toward Malcolm, Ben placed his fingers on the same spellcards and let the energy flow through him.

Malcolm let the howling balls fly.

The orangey-mint combo barely registered Ben his mouth and nose before he leapt.

The violet globes broke open, blossoming into rolling conflagrations of purple doom.

Ben thumbed *Pop* and channeled into it. In a flurry of tiny bubbles, Ben's low-level teleportation spell raised him higher, allowing him to slide across the top of the flames that continued under him as though he were surfing the fire.

Ben landed before the balls completely dissipated behind him. "Do you bend?" He pointed at Malcolm, slid his finger to *Blast*, and warned. "I still have plenty of power."

Malcolm's stomach remained devoid of Krotosian magic. Still he raised his chin in defiance.

None of his other chakras are open. He's totally out of magic. Ben checked his Anvilsmith. *Sixty-seven awatts left. Good.* Ben stopped jogging. His *Usain* spell ended. *I can't fire on a defenseless caster.*

Ben lowered his arm.

Malcolm's lips arced up and parted in the single smile Ben disliked the most in the world.

It was the same one Ben had looked up to see after being hooked for the first time in Adept Love's class on the Monday following his loss of his thirteenth birthday school gifts. Embarrassed at having to return the two gifts he didn't lose, Ben had been trying to avoid the other students when something cold and green cut into his forearm. He had seen lines drawn between casters in practice, but never knew—never would've guessed—that there was a hook on the end. That tiny hook had landed clean. There hadn't been any blood where it landed, but the pain of his mystic self being pierced forced an almost helpless yelp.

Ben had become still and hoped the pain would, too. Adept Love would be over to him in a moment and—it ripped up his arm. He had belted a ragged cry as the hook tore through him, rounding his shoulder to slide down his chest, and pulse against his sternum. Ben hadn't recalled hitting the gym floor, but when his senses returned, he'd been on his knees and doubled over. Malcolm—*that lousy smile*—had stood over him, chiding, "Welcome to the real world. Man up. Quit crying, baby."

Recalling—and seeing—the same smug mug, green

energy flashed through Ben as his emotions flared. A soccer-ball-sized blast of green energy—containing his full arcane flow—flew from his hand. It rocketed across the desert, crackling as the dirt and rocks beneath were highlighted with emerald menace.

Malcolm's smile faded and his eyes widened. He tried to dodge.

Too late.

The energy crashed into him and launched him backward. Holding his chest, Malcolm got to a knee and struggled to his feet. He lifted his chin again.

Ben bellowed and let another crackling blast fly.

This time, Malcolm pushed his chest toward the spell—and was thrown further.

Malcolm rose to a knee. Blood coated his trembling lips as they worked up to smile.

No, you don't get to smile! Ben let loose again. *Not now!*

The green power lit Malcolm's body as he fell back and slid across the dirt. Weakly, he said. "I bend."

The Anvilsmith pinged, Tex's voice echoed through. "Confirmed. He relented."

Don't care! Ben sneered.

Lost.

Enraged.

Nilosian energy flashed through Ben. Five sizzling spheres rocked and curved at Malcolm; their wake sucked little light there was from the night.

Malcolm's head started to lift.

Lips pressed tight, Ben struggled. A part of him didn't want to dismiss the spell, but—*he relented*—he came to his senses and dismissed the black energy.

The phantom wisps formed a hand and lurched to grab at Malcolm's throat—

A memory—defiant Nilosian teeth biting and breaking Jack's bloody arm. The thief's bellow—flashed. Ben grabbed his forehead. Fear of murder —*murderer!*—turned the breath in his chest to ice. *Oh shit, what have I done?*

The hand gripped Malcolm's throat.

Malcolm gasped and grabbed at his neck.

No!

The hand dissipated.

Ben exhaled hard. He placed his shaking hands on his weak knees and tried to steady himself. *Almost killed him.* He took a trembling inhalation. *Breathe, Ben.* The air, as though afraid of what lay inside him, stuttered through his throat and into his lungs. *Just breathe. In. Out. Just like that. In, and out.* Breath started to come easier.

Malcolm groaned and flopped over.

Concern—*how bad did I hurt him?*—framed Ben's features as he hustled over to where the Dunn-Blatt writhed ever so slowly. *Well, he's able to move…*

Malcolm's voice warbled and faded as he said, "Copy any ability you want from me, take spells, but," Malcolm drew a wet breath. His air flow strengthened to plead, "Please give me my hook back. It's a family heirloom."

Enchanted sight still keen, Ben scanned the desert for the Nilosians. They were gone. He asked, "Who rode here with you?"

"Huh?" Malcolm looked bewildered.

"Your car." Ben went to point at the passenger door

that had been left open to find it closed. "Who else came with you?"

"What are you talking about?" The Dunn-Blatt rolled over onto his stomach. Scrunching up to his hands and knees, he croaked, "I—" He sighed. "I am alone."

"Very well." Ben examined the desert again, slower this time and still could not find them. *Too bad Tex couldn't verify either of them.* "Get up." Ben went and sat in his car. As he waited for Malcolm to collect himself, he put the top up, and turned on the heater.

Malcolm got back to his feet. "My hook?"

I need time to think and being on the road to Meadows Towing isn't the place for it. Ben started his Transcend. "Follow me to the festival. I'll have an answer for you there."

Chapter Thirty-Nine

GOODBYE MR. NICE GUY

WELL AFTER 4 A.M., the mundane parking lot had emptied out. Ben and Malcolm walked to the entrance —dark from the outside—in silence. All the while, Ben held the nail in his palm alternating between squeezing it and holding it loose. The closer to the entrance they got, the tighter he had to grip it as guilt—*it's not yours*— kept pressuring him to turn it loose.

The early morning air remained still and cold. Ben found his elbows tight against his sides, trying to retain some of his body heat. Like a punch, the fragrant Samhain Festival popcorn—*it'd be hot, buttery goodness in my stomach*—assaulted his nose making his mouth water and empty gut rumble. *You're purposefully not thinking about the Dunn-Blatt's family heirloom.* Ben nodded to the realization. His guilt wrestled with getting vindication for everyone who'd fell prey to the *former* bully.

He and Malcolm came to a stop just outside the fairgrounds. At the threshold, muffled shouts and laughs from dozens of spell duels bled through the silencing enchantment. *How much Mystique*—Ben's wondering thought got derailed—*Wow, Malcolm's bowing his head…*

Everyone inside would see the acknowledgment of being bettered and rumors would fly about what had transpired to make a notoriously unabashed—even by Dunn-Blatt standards—student publicly admit to being bested by another in front of everyone participating in the Samhain Shenanigans. *They're going to wonder who I am and how I bested him. Luckily, all APA students have been segregated to only duel near the smelly Mystic Menagerie and I'm not wearing my school uniform. Only me and Malcolm—and those two Nilosians—know the whole story.*

"My tether?" Malcolm kept his neck bent and swallowed hard. "Please?"

The faint shouts from within the fairgrounds had grown silent. *They've stopped their duels to watch this? Goodness.* Shocked at being at the center of attention, and Malcolm asking in front of everyone, Ben almost pulled the nail form his pocket. He let go and his hand came out empty. "No."

The Dunn-Blatt pulled up his hood and touched the center dangling over his forehead. A magical darkness filled the space, shrouding Malcolm's face.

Oh, man. Ben dove his hand back into his pocket. *Am I being fair?* He gripped the hook, and let it fall again. "If you keep my identity and my abilities to yourself, I will return it to you in a year and a day." *Anyone would call that fair.*

Malcolm nodded. Grateful in not getting his way, his voice came out meek and wet. "Thank you."

He seems really sorry. Ben tensed his neck to keep unbidden word—words of instant forgiveness—from passing through. *If I say them, I'll hand it over.* To get his hand away from the nail, Ben undid his top button and rubbed his throat to ease the building discomfort. *Stick with your decision.* Ben patted Malcolm on the back. "Until then, Malcolm, practice without tethers. It will make you a better caster."

The Dunn-Blatt nodded as he entered the fairgrounds.

Near starving, Ben got in his car and, for the last time that night, left the festival.

Chapter Forty

(IN) THE END

A FEW HOURS LATER, as Ben was about to fall asleep, Toad called on his Anvilsmith wanting to meet at Meadows Towing to talk business before sunrise that morning. Not exactly sure what they could possibly have to discuss, and reluctant to ever go out to Meadows Towing again, Ben insisted they meet in the city, at noon.

Now, with the Las Vegas sun high above and mundane traffic humming past, blissfully ignorant of the school of magic, Ben stood in the Archon Private Academy parking lot.

Though they had originally set a meeting spot near the Samhain Festival, Ben had made a last-minute location change to have the orcs—Toad and Jek only—come here so he would be able to see an ambush or assault being staged before it unfolded. Relieved that the Komir necklace had awakened with the rising sun, Ben rubbed it to activate the totem's shielding charm as a lone Meadows Towing truck clattered into the lot. He anchored the necklace to draw from his mostly recovered Argosian reserve.

Ben raised a hand to have the tow truck stop before the first speed bump. He wanted them far away from him and his car. Also, Ben didn't want to give away Tex's position when he whispered, "Remember the plan."

His companion's voice and syntax had returned to its synthesized norm shortly after the duel and the robot replied from where he had clamped himself onto the car's front fender. Tex said, "Barring an EMP, I am unable to forget."

Ben walked toward the tow truck. Jek sat behind the wheel with Toad in the passenger seat. Both wore thick sunglasses as though they were recovering from a late night of partying.

Toad, the shaman, got out. Though Ben wouldn't have been surprised if they both had been wearing black armor, the light green orc wore the standard Meadow's Towing t-shirt, blue jeans, and black boots. Also walking across the lot, Toad raised his thick hand to the top edge of his sunglasses to further shade his eyes from the midday sun. The orc raised his chin and uttered hearty grunts, speaking in the Giant's tongue. Toad asked, "Everything all right, Bastion?"

Ben didn't answer until he moved to stand fifty-feet —*a good dueling range*—away. "My name is Ben."

Toad lowered his eyes to a point between the two of them and extended his palms in a slow, supplicating fashion. He didn't want to fight. Toad switched to English. "Twice apologize, Might-Fist. Just following your last orders."

Why is he calling me Might-Fist? Ben walked forward and asked, "I told you to call me Bastion?"

"Yes." Toad's eyes adjusted to remain focused on a near-precise center between them as Ben moved forward. "And to speak Giant."

Ben stopped twenty-feet away. Any closer and he couldn't lock the orc into a duel. "When did I do this?"

"During the Ur-Krurkson feast. Two nights ago." Toad raised his eyes to meet Ben's but kept his arms wide and palms up to the sky. "After you defeated Ur-Krurk's son and took mastership over his forces."

Ben's brow furrowed. "So, you're saying I won?"

Toad nodded.

Ben asked, "Then why was I strapped to the bed?"

"None of us understood it, but—" Toad lowered his eyes to the center point between them. "Again, Might-Fist, only by your exact orders."

Ben asked, "Why were there goblins in the building?"

"They are yours." Toad paused to deepen his bow as far as he could and still retain the ability to make eye contact. "We bought the first one to clean around Meadows Towing. The second was property of Ur-Krurkson and, thus, part of your spoils."

Ben touched his *Orion* spellcard and channeled Argosian energy. Abe and Oscar appeared in red flashes. Both had their, now signature, weapons. Ben motioned Toad to stand. "One last question. If I won, why was the would-be victory meal be called the *Ur-Krurkson feast*?"

"Because, Might-Fist—" A proud, satisfied grin spread the orc's mouth as it straightened. That smile was the first Ben had seen from any of them. Toad enthusiastically rubbed his belly with both hands. "We feasted on Ur-Krurk's son."

Recalling his upset stomach and the haunting onion taste, Ben's facial features slacked. "I ate—" Blood retreated from his extremities, his gorge began to rise, and his stomach lurched. "I ate someone?"

Toad's delighted nod held too much enjoyment.

Ben's stomach heaved again. He turned away to throw up, but managed to hold his breakfast in.

Toad continued, "Don't worry, Might-Fist…"

Something very much like horror of what he would hear next filled Ben. He dared to look at the thrilled orc. Concerned, Toad had extended his arms as if to lend strength from a distance. *At least it feels like he's trying to help.*

Trying to console him, Toad earnestly swore, "You only had the best parts."

The information bowled Ben over. His stomach gave a mighty kick and he couldn't hold his sic back. Once he recovered, Ben thanked Toad for coming, then sent the orcs away so he could wonder—with true horror—at what Bastion had done while in control of his body.

Back in his car, Ben pulled his Anvilsmith and sat it on his. With his camera app open, he stopped to put his nerves in check and let his gaze search the light blue sky for any daytime stars. There were none. Ben took a deep breath. *Whatever I see is not my doing.* His attention on the device, his finger hovered over play. *It may be my body, but these are not* my *deeds.* He nodded to reaffirm the mental avowal and pressed play.

THE VIDEO mostly showed the inside of his coat, but the audio was complete. He whispered "go" to his orcs. He and Ur-Krurk's son exchanged words as his own voice growled and struggled before Bastion took control and gave his declaration.

Then the time for words was over. There were a few flashes of combat when his coat flapped open, but Ben found both his hands clenched tight against the sounds of the fevered pitch of battle. There had been some gunfire at the beginning, but everything soon devolved into clangs, grunts, screams, and curses.

Somehow worse than the sounds of killing and dying, hearing his voice uttering constant strings of sentences in a language he didn't know. It sounded similar to the hiss-gargles he had heard in Pepperjacks when the big red fist had knocked the doors from its hinges. The voice, then, had been thunderous. The words coming from his own mouth, commandeered by Bastion, failed to match that trumpeting volume, but they were being spat with unequaled venom.

Then.

Silence.

The profound quiet didn't last. Groans warbled up and someone gibbered softly.

Footsteps—his footsteps—as Bastion walked around repeatedly asking in Giant, "Will you blood-oath?" Eight had said no and, after each negative answer, his voice whispered in the hiss-gargle language. Then, fierce bellowing shrieks screamed out and became silent. From the ninth on, every voice answered yes to the question.

His voice called for a fire pit.

He gave a speech about how the mighty had fallen...about how he would enact a ritual that would make the victors become mightier by consuming their fallen foes...about reaping hidden powers from flesh and soul.

Bastion then changed back to the hiss-gargle language. He rattled on for a good ten minutes before calling, in the Giant's tongue, to start to the Ur-Krurkson feast.

Those remaining exploded into cheers. There were chopping sounds. Ripping sounds. Chomping sounds.

"I choose you to be my trusted ally here," Bastion said quietly. "As such, consume this heart and this mind, and reap with me."

Also in Giant, a voice, deeper than any orc's —*probably one of the tuzvuls*—replied, "My honor is yours."

Cheer rose. The disgusting sounds continued as orcs called which body parts they wanted until the video stopped.

BEN LOWERED HIS HEAD.

My Krotosian magic and regeneration... A numbing revulsion washed over him. *Bastion enacted a mystic ritual, and consumed Ur-Krurk's son. That's—* Wanting to hide from his revelation, Ben covered his face with his hands. *That's why I have these abilities.* He recalled his excitement at his ankle healing and shame struck. *I had been so excited. Then Alice—* "Alice." Her disgusted expression and her sudden aversion rang back. *When she said she smelled death, her olfactory glands must've picked up the ogre's demise on my breath, but only once we were face-to-face without the wind whipping the odor away...*

Ben thought about deleting the video, but—until the sun went down—he simply sat there. Stunned.

WHEN HE HAD RETURNED HOME, his dad had looked him over, gave him an approving, conspiratorial wink and suggested he get some sleep. Figuring his father made up a story to appease his mom—who had always been the disciplinarian. When he woke, Ben didn't question his parents' suggestion that he return to the Samhain Festival to observe the closing celebration. In the past, he had been only allowed one night and, last year, they had even allowed him to pick an evening other than the last night. Though his last year's trench coat was tight across the shoulders, Ben wore it to be in school colors.

Late—*again*—he had to park way out in the mundane lot—*again*. An orchestra played as a fireworks array pierced the fairgrounds sky.

Mundanes *oohed* and *ahhed*.

Ben turned his eyes skyward and found a relatively bland display.

He refused to slow at the line of *Shame on Sam Hain* protestors and ran with such abandon, that they hurried to get out of his way. Nearly reckless, he occasionally bumped into people in his rush through the mundane part of the fairgrounds to get to the open starwise viewing grounds.

Panting, Ben held his sides as he jogged to the edge of the open field, then had to watch where he moved as thousands of casters had gathered to take in the show. They covered the grass—almost all the way to the entrance—with a multitude of colored blankets, as families *ohhed* and *ahhed*.

Appreciative, he smiled, nodded, and bowed his apologies as he squeezed his way along the perimeter.

Here the mystic pyrotechnics seemed to split the sky open in vibrant colors which blossomed riotously in the night sky.

He leaned against the exterior chain-link fence and clapped with everyone else when three great rockets shot into the sky and opened with a cacophony to release three dragons made of fireworks. Circling high, the red, white, and black dragons in the festival colors also embodied the three most powerful colors of magic.

Readying for a grand mock battle where the red would doubtlessly win, again—*as it always dose*—the dragons began to vie for position.

Other latecomers trickled in, brushing by him to fill the remaining area.

Keeping one hand on his spellcard holder and the other on his Anvilsmith, Ben ignored them as the red dragon and white dragon teamed up to attack the black dragon.

Though the black is bigger this year, that's hardly fair. Still, he cheered with everyone else at the spectacular aerial display.

A set of arms slid along his flanks inside his coat. A soft body pressed into him. Hands climbed up his in a familiar fashion.

About to shove the person away, Ben recognized the

owner of brown eyes and blonde hair. He flushed. His pulse quickened.

"I've been looking for you." Clarissa tiptoed and kissed him.

Mmm, cotton candy.

She said, "I'm glad you finally came back."

Ben had questions. Foremost of which was how she came to be sealed in a burlap bag in Old Henderson. But instead of asking the series of questions he had planned and prepared for, he wrapped his arms around her, and they went back to kissing.

The three energy sources in his body heated and swelled, along with his blood, making this wonderful moment sort of uncomfortable. The Nilosian whirlpool in his head rocked the worst. Thunderous booms—*too loud*—from the sky thumped against the blood in his ears. Timed with the explosions above, his three energy sources became still and he focused on enjoying Clarissa's cotton-candied lips.

They took a break.

He looked at her as she smiled looked up at the show. Amazingly, her brown eyes changed to a light violet and her blonde hair took on a silvery glow.

What had been cheers turned to horrified shrieks.

Why are they freaking out? Ben pulled Clarissa closer as people scattered, stealing fearful glances over their shoulders at the sky.

He turned his eyes skyward.

The red dragon had its head bowed. Next to it, the white dragon's body—*the white dragon never dies*—snapped and fizzled to nothing. *Whoa! That's why.* Many used the battle as an indicator of the year to come. *It's just a show.*

Triumphant, and spewing red pyrotechnic flame toward the field, the firework black dragon's eye sockets had formed rolling dark-purple orbs with menacing green irises, which scanned the field. As though honing in, the gaze racked over him and Clarissa a few times. To stand his ground, Ben told himself again, *It's just a show.*

Amidst the unending booms—booms so hard they registered on his skin—Ben noticed a suck of wind on his coat.

Swirling gray robes appeared before the Vibrosian Primary materialized. She grabbed Clarissa, pulled her away from his grip, and—before Ben could reach out to grab Clarissa back—spun her robes to disappear with Clarissa in tow.

One of the few not running for cover, Ben watched the two remaining dragons explode into thousands of roman candles.

Walking to his car, Ben tucked his hands into his pockets and, basked in the afterglow of cotton-candied lips. *Best night yet.*

BEN SAT on the back of his car, looking at Pepperjacks. Though the mundane papers said there had been a devastating fire here, mystic artisans had obviously been at work.

Tinted glass had been put in place on the front doors and would keep sunlight from flowing through. The valet awning had been rebuilt, with new ivory columns standing where the old ones had been. Even the deep red paint, which gave the building a brick-like appearance from a distance, had been reapplied.

He put his tablet away.

Clarissa hadn't responded to his texts and he'd even tried calling her number, again, and it rang to voicemail, again. For the week following the Samhain Festival, Ben had tried to connect with her daily, but had been unable to reach her. After the first week, he tried every Friday after school let out. Still nothing. He never got to ask her how she came to be in the burlap bag in the first place or why the Primary took her away.

His eyes flew open and he grabbed his jaw in sudden realization. *Has she been recaptured? If so—* Relenting to his lack of information or leads, Ben heaved a sigh. *If so, there's nothing I can do about it. Heck, if she is missing, I don't even know anyone to ask. And if I did, they'd probably suspect me!*

Though Papa Mojo said they weren't going to get together, Ben felt Clarissa—like Jek—was one of the few people true to themselves. Then again, the diviner could've lied about that too.

With Winter break here, Ben had been hoping to spend some time with her. He still had no idea what a proper Yule gift would be, but enjoyed the thought of exchanging seasonal gifts with her. Due to her lack of any kind of reply, Ben really wanted to forget her, but his dreams often centered on kissing her. When the dreams turned to nightmares, they would end with him touching Penelope's hand. And Alice... Well, he just tried not to think about her, as his thoughts would jump to—and focus on—how she reacted to him after the battle and what her sister tried to do to him. Their hissing to each other rang back. *Wonder what she said about me?*

Trying to put it all out of his head—for now—Ben read the new marquee under the Pepperjacks' sign. *Open next October.* "It looks to be ready now."

Even though he'd probably only get a handshake for his efforts—*better than trying to turn me to stone*—Ben really wanted to return the Node Key. It had been a nagging concern when he believed he had lost to Ur-Krurk's son and, if he had, the ogre would have gained much more than Meadows Towing.

Ben heaved a sigh and climbed over the bags of winnings from his Conjurer's Course to drop into the driver's seat. Earlier in the week—as they would every year—Samhain Festival employees had delivered all items lost during the Shenanigans as well as delivering unclaimed prizes.

Wary of his SD cards, Ben took them to Crystal, the only diviner he knew who would give a straight answer, to see if—possibly courtesy of Collins—they were cursed. She said they were clean, so he had picked them up before driving to Pepperjacks.

Looking forward to a long week of joyful tinkering in his Meadows Towing basement lab, Ben drove away with a small smile.

ABOUT THE AUTHOR

Ezekiel James Boston hales from Las Vegas and currently resides in the Great Northwest. Favoring fantasy, science fiction, and paranormal occult, he's authored over a hundred short stories, a score of short novels, and half a dozen full length novels.

Aside from being an avid writer, Ezekiel enjoys reading and games of all sorts. He chose to give up "active" sports after jamming his fingers and discovering that an author cannot slam their forehead onto the keyboard and have the story appear on the screen.

For exclusive content, please visit:
ezekieljamesboston.com/subscribe-to-ejb/

ALSO BY EZEKIEL JAMES BOSTON

Novels:

Birthday Bedlam: Book One

Samhain Shenanigans: Book Two

Yuletide Yield: Book Three

Novelette:

Nexus Bar & Grill: A World of Benjamin Baxter Starwise
Novelette

Short stories:

Gateway Blood, Buck Tales

Soul Survivor, Buck Tales

Jamal & the Skeleton's Heart, Buck Tales

Collections:

Benjamin Baxter — Darkness Within Trilogy

COMING SOON

Samhain Shenanigans, Book Two of The Darkness Within Trilogy

Please note: Word of mouth is crucial for any author to succeed. If you enjoyed this book, please consider rating it or leaving a review where you purchased... Even if it's just a line or two.

Thank you for reading.